## BY MARTIN COPELAND

*The Boys from Dogtown*
*LA Love Stories*
*Manhunt in France*

PHOTOPLAYS
*River of Doubt*
*Right Proud: the Buffalo Soldiers*

# GRAND CANYON

## A Novel

Martin Copeland

RAINBOW BRIDGE

ISBN: 978-1-7366689-5-5
Rainbow Bridge Books

# CONTENTS

# GRAND CANYON

## PART 1

## Dawn

A solitary eagle floated on wind currents, looking for prey even this early as brilliant rays of light banished darkness and another day began to dawn over one of the most magnificent spectacles of color and stone on earth. Ray after ray illuminated the kaleidoscope colors of promontories, buttes and cliffs, shafting gold into the whorling sandstone depths of what men have decided, most aptly, to call the Grand Canyon.

Most days the eagle had the panorama to himself. Some tourists make the effort to rise and sunrise, snapping photos from barriered rim viewpoints and breathing even while affirming the view "breathtaking," but their numbers scarcely fill a breadbasket and the astonishing sights, always different with the ever-changing interplay of light and cloud, pass as another memorable moment in time reserved for the few. Even fewer repeat the experience.

One who did, virtually every dawn, had bivouacked—somehow—on a narrow ledge just wide enough for his sleeping bag and camp stove, perched precariously at his side. His legs dangled over the rim, over 5,000 feet of descent to the Colorado River below. As the eagle glided above and dipped down toward the Canyon's South Rim above, he raised his coffee in salute. "Good morning, *Atsah*."

The Watcher had had a long and busy night, but he tried to manage his life so as to never miss a canyon sunrise. He watched each angle and reflection on the great Canyon with an appreciation that went beyond aesthetic. One might call it love.

He'd been awarded the monicker "Insane Zane" for his penchant to take risks, as per now, when most people, even experienced climbers, would find it one hell of a risk to find a way back from this ledge up to the rim. Not to mention, the way down.

But Zane Bailey was not insane in the clinical sense. Some people knew that and had long ago stopped making excuses for him.

The big-ass SUV motored past the Grand Canyon Park boundary, past the small town with private dwellings that had been permitted and since, tolerated by all but a few hardcore environmentalists—"fanatics," the SUV driver called them, including and especially Zane Bailey—toward an area of private construction that hadn't yet been approved.

But the driver, Muir Wilson, was confident it would be and construction zones had already been laid out. She'd been moving faster  than authorized limits, as she did in much of her life, so when she rolled up to the small prefab hut that housed her company's night security guard, the SUV kicked up a bunch of dust and gravel that sprayed onto the hut's siding.

Muir hopped out and strode fast to meet Clyde, the guard who came quickly from what would be the first subdivision site for future homes. They would not have a full canyon view, as homes perched right on the rim would need a special dispensation. The property was owned and paid for by her stepfather, however, and Muir was also confident that this dispensation would be accorded. It sufficed to bend ears of the right people, or sometimes, right person, and that challenge had been inserted prominently  on her week's program.

Those homes would cost a fortune and make for a money tree that kept on growing year after year. As she well knew from her youth and heritage, once man altered his natural earth environment, it was very hard, and frequently impossible, to restore it to what it had once been.

As per the towering pines that had already been cut and trimmed, huge logs now bordering the site, forming a kind of barrier. What to do with them? That hadn't yet been placed on the agenda. She'd find a solution in good time, which she usually didn't have much of in a crowded, busy life.

Muir was in her '20s, the kind of natural beauty that did honor to a youth spent mostly outdoors. She hiked, worked out, and got plenty of exercise sifting through suitors who often stared at her on first sight like encountering a Canyon puma up close and personal. She would often mentally quip, "Boing!" when one such's eyeballs popped, as always making it hard to get the admirer to concentrate on real estate business.

Muir was as charming when she needed to be as she was beautiful, and really only one man had ever seemed armor-plated against her attractions. A fanatical environmentalist. Against all her efforts to resist getting irritated by this fact, and him, he set her off and the wrong kind of sparks flew. The Grand Canyon's brush and forest presented a constant fire hazard, a potential natural catastrophe, and when she and the "eco-freak" were together—which she avoided most mightily—the same kind of conflagration loomed ever present and possible.

Today Muir wasn't dressed as usual in a serious business woman's skirt, blouse and heels. She'd paired designer jeans with mucho expensive leather boots, a Western-style bangled shirt and a yellow bandanna, and tied her hair back. She looked fit to ride cowgirl in a rodeo, and in fact, she'd been there, done that. More than once she'd been selected Queen of rodeos, all around the country. But that was in a past she preferred to forget.

The roughhewn guard Clyde who greeted her was impressed, but knew she was all business and didn't dare flatter.

"Morning, Clyde."

"Didn't expect you this early, Miss Wilson. You beat the roosters."

"Big event this morning. Kind of a homecoming. No vandalism last night? Like maybe when you drifted off to sleep?"

Clyde was taken aback, royally.

"Why, no m'am. Check the video if you don't trust in me. I made my rounds like always. Anybody sneak in here, he'd have to be some kind of special operator. All I heard was coyotes."

"Some coyotes have human names, Clyde. I know you do your job as best you can. Come along."

She motioned and they started walking toward the site entrance where there was a big billboard.

"Like when I'm camping. Must have spent half my girlhood in a tent. You wake up in the morning and fix yourself a coffee, and breathe good, haul out your breakfast, look out and watch dawnlight hit the canyons or mountain, and just in that instant a raven swoops down and grabs your muffin. I can tell you they prefer blueberry, but any kind's fair pickings. Check. They don't play fair."

It took Clyde just a second to get her meaning, and by the time he did they'd come in full view of the billboard, a florid poster of the Grand Canyon at its finest, most touristy panorama in background, modern Western-style homes in foreground, and a blurb blazoning "PARADISE ESTATES. Homes Grander than the Canyon."

Muir indicated it with a nod, and Clyde's eyes moved down from the name and slogan to a piece of hand-drawn graffiti--real artwork, actually.

The drawing was in color, an excellent reproduction of the famous Coppertone sun-lotion girl, with her derrière partly exposed and drawers slipped halfway off—except where in the classic ads her sunburned fanny suffered from lack of protection, here it was about to be bitten by a mischievous gila monster.

Clyde was appalled.

"How in the hell…now Miss Wilson…"

"No apologies, Clyde. A cockroach can sneak past anybody if he's quick enough. Except this one can draw."

"If I catch whoever that bastard is—"

"Leave him to me. I know where to look. Or should I say, smell."

On the ledge where he'd gotten minimal shuteye, Zane Bailey finished loading his backpack by rolling up a pair of paintbrushes. No White Spirit had touched them, and they stuck heartily to their wrappings. Very soon they would be added to a recycle bin expressly designated for this kind of "special" waste product.

Zane shouldered his pack, took a last look at the canyon, and began freeclimbing the rock cliff up toward the rim. No vertiginous spectators needed apply for the show as he inched up, precarious handhold by precarious handhold.

Time would tell if he made it to the top for a special ceremony he planned to crash.

## A New Leader Arrives

Tanner Overlook had been chosen by outgoing Head Park Ranger Clarence Hillis, whitehaired under his widebrimmed Ranger hat, for his farewell ceremony. Such as it was. He was an economical man, and he'd served his country efficiently and well as head boss of the famous national park.

It had to be as early as dawnlight would allow, because as always, Grand Canyon park Rangers had a myriad of duties and tasks great and small that day and any day. They would be about their business as soon as gemütlichkeit and outgoing and incoming speeches allowed.

Not every Ranger could be present at this South Rim ceremony, because the Canyon could never be left unattended, but many were there to hear their soon-to-be-former boss address the group  Rangers who'd been under his command for many distinguished years.

A wonderland of dawning colors formed the backdrop to a makeshift dais as Clarence Hillis intoned like the satisfied man he was, leaving a world of responsibility 24/24 for R&R: "For 20 years this magnificent canyon has been my real home. Going to be hard to leave it but life moves on, like me and Jeannie. We'll be heading down Tucson way and the desert—-flat desert."

That drew chuckles from the group. "Gonna miss you all. Each and every one of you. Even the ones I butted heads with. Like those old billygoats who come round our campsites every now and then and scrounge for grub some careless campers leave around. Lucinda, gotta thank you for taking it upon yourself to handle them. It's a thankless job and we Rangers've got lots of those, but that one's no picnic for the olfactories. Maybe that's why you came to this Canyon built up and stayed built up. Wrestling those billygoats."

Lucinda Devere, the "built up" Amazon Hillis had in his sights, chuckled along with her colleagues who knew better than not to chuckle along with her. She was as right about the proper route to scale a cliff or negotiate a boulder field as she was often wrong about the men she chose to hike with through life.

Hillis turned his gaze toward a ranger who gave "lean and hungry" new meaning.

"Harvey," Hillis said, "we're gonna be down there in the low desert where there's more kinds of cactus than there are rocks. What am I gonna do without a man who can tell you more about nuts and berries than you'd ever want to know? Not to mention—well, soon as you introduced yourself as Harvey Pine, 'like the tree,' I knew we had a man on our team who could explain the natural world like it <u>needed</u> explaining."

He inserted a pregnant pause.

"At length."

This drew laughter from the group who knew Harvey's wind was as long as the one that blew from the West.

Lincoln Williams offered with a wry smile, "Well sir, this canyon's taken millions of years to form…"

More laughter.

Harvey protested, "In all my talks, I have never seen a campfire go out. Now that is physical and chronometric proof."

Blake Wilson, a man in his fifties, the very definition of "ruggedly handsome," smiled along with all his new charges.

Hillis continued, "Take care of yourself and our visitors like you always do, Lincoln. You had some growing pains but I can assure you, Blake, he's grown. We're entering a violent future, I'm afraid. Folks crossing boundaries and not caring if they do or who gets hurt."

"Nothing we can't handle, sir," Lincoln assured.

"You and Josh came to our canyon from the mean streets and still don't much like taking orders. But you do take them and I was always glad. Even if it took a hell of a lot of persuasion sometimes."

Josh Allen had the look and accent of a New York City boy, if there was a Big Apple look. And if there wasn't, no matter because he was proud of his concrete roots. He nodded, recognizing the justice of what Hillis said.

Clarence turned his gaze on Lily Dawnwind of the Havasu tribe.

"Thanks so much for coming, Lily."

She had dressed in ceremonial garb, striking colors that competed with the canyon colors beginning to blaze as the morning sun rose higher. She acknowledged Hillis' sincerity with a response in her native tongue that even if he didn't understand it exactly, echoed with warmth.

Hillis turned to a girl younger than everyone, looking as if she was fresh out of college. Which she was.

"Missy, our latest intern. Keep up the tradition, okay?"

She smiled and nodded.

Clarence turned toward Blake Wilson.

"And now, this old soldier's fading away so a new man can come into the spotlight. And I think you'll see, he's made for it. He started his career here and everywhere he's gone since then, whatever park in whatever state, he left it better than how he found it. Park and state, if you want my opinion. He'd make a hell of a governor. But we're glad we got him, and let's make sure we keep him by serving with competence, pride and dedication. Ladies and gentlemen, Mr. Blake Wilson."

Hillis' successor had been turning his eagle eye on everyone. In his case, Hillis' praise was no mere floral words, but accurate—Wilson could pilot a Piper or Boeing, chopper or glider with equal assurance, blessed as he was with exceptional vision and the kind of right stuff that made flying machines purr with calm and efficiency.

He could have had a lucrative career as chief man in a cockpit, but flying, he said once to his active, relentlessly questioning daughter before she left his day-to-day life, posed one great, unacceptable problem. It put him high and far above the landscapes of canyon, mountain and meadow that he loved, no matter how technology and satellite photos brought them into highlight.

He didn't care for highlights. He craved total immersion, up close and personal. He'd had to sacrifice, most heartbreaking of all, a wife who didn't share his passion for the outdoors, and preserving it more than her, she felt. Perhaps accurately. Finally she'd wrenched his daughter from arms and his hearth, which was no hearth at all because constantly changing as Blake went from park to park across the American wilds that still remained in the late 20th and early 21st century.

Blake Wilson had devoted his life to preserving and protecting those lands, and now one of them, maybe the greatest, had been placed in his hands.

He'd hoped, without really deep down believing, that his daughter would welcome him along with his Rangers this bright and beautiful morning, but as he scanned the group, he only saw his future partner employees. As Hillis cited them, he made mental notes of what the outgoing chief said, and vowed to learn each man and woman's strengths and weaknesses and most of all, backgrounds. He'd had his own ups and downs and knew how they molded a personality. The people who came to the Canyon for brief stays or longer were as varied as the world, and it took all types to manage their visits. He liked the urban echoes that Lincoln and Josh brought to his team, the passion that Harvey  lived and breathed, the potential he could see already in an intern like Missy, Lucinda's cool and presence, the blend of tradition and modern that he felt Lily Dawnwind would display as they together sought to manage the claims of past and future.

As Wilson stepped to the dais, shaking hands warmly with Hillis, he gave him a wide smile and warm hug.

"Thank you Clarence. And thank you for all the years you've given heart and soul to this Canyon, these Rangers, and the people who come here from all over the world."

He led the group in applauding Hillis who had joined his wife Jeannie, she not succeeding in holding back tears.

When the ovation subsided, Wilson raised his eyes and let his regard roam over the assembled men and women.

"Ladies, gentlemen, you know as well as I do that some of your colleagues couldn't make it here this morning because their schedules wouldn't permit it. Too many tourists to guide and inform, too many campsites to survey, too many backcountry trails needing repair. You all are here because your shifts start later, and let me say, I look forward to sitting down and getting to know each and every one of you. When our schedules permit. You'll find out real quick I'm not one for speeches. I'm for getting things done—the right way. We have a United States Senator visiting us this week. We've got his attention for one solid day. Let's make our case, show what we do. But as you all know, he's only one of thousands and every single one of them counts for us and on us. I'm proud to be working with you and for them. Keep me proud. Starting now."

Midway through his discourse, Wilson's voice had lifted into even brighter sunlight than what was now hitting the canyon's brilliant rock colors, because he saw a woman striding quickly from the parking lot, looking beautiful in her leather and yellow bandanna—Muir, his daughter.

She'd come, after all. And even though he'd wished upon her star ever since the US government had called from Washington to announce his transfer, he was still surprised that the star had fallen at this moment at this corner of the Canyon.

Just momentarily as he wound up, he thought he'd mistaken her arrival because his hyper-keen eyes spotted her scowling. Maybe she'd come not to praise Caesar but bury him?

But no. She was scowling—and that seemed too mild a word—at a rather disheveled man with a ragged backpack and look even more, heading the same way she was headed. Which she clearly appreciated not one bit.

Blake knew the Hermit Trail began some distance away from where the backpacker had come, and his logic born from a lifetime's experience on the trail told him the newcomer had scrambled up the cliff from the canyon No ordinary man could do that, he knew, and from the looks some of his Rangers who'd remarked his presence tossed his way, punctuated by a few ironic smiles, he figured, this was a black sheep.

And just like that Blake Wilson left off, stepping down to shake hands with Clarence and hug his wife. Everybody understood the ceremony was over. The Rangers started milling around, exchanging small talk.

Harvey turned to Josh, worried.

"He won't cut out my campfire programs, will he? He didn't make a commitment. I was expecting a commitment."

"Harvey, government's cutting back everywhere," Josh didn't reassure. "Why do you think a US Senator is coming?"

"We sing songs and everything. It's interactive!"

"Let's just hope he won't want to build a dam smack in the middle of the Canyon."

"They'd never do that. That's an entire ecosystem."

"For people like the Senator, eco means economic. Period."

Wilson began moving through the group, pressing the flesh with each Ranger.

Zane Bailey moved over to Muir, who was staring at Hillis and ignoring him, so he provoked her as usual: "Tucson. He bought a tract home, paid way too much. You make the deal?"

"Not my territory."

"Like here. Didn't expect to see you."

"He's my father."

"You remembered. How long since you've seen him?"

"That's none of your business. Asshole."

"You've grown some thorns. Real prickly pear."

"Good for when I meet a prick. And put this in your lawless brain, if you have one: from now on, our security guards will be carrying a weapon."

"Harming wildlife in a national park is a federal offense."

"We'll just be removing trash. Quite beneficial for the park ecosystem. And our property."

Blake came up, fostering a truce just before the blows commenced.

"God I'm glad to see you."

Meaning of course, Muir. They exchanged a really heartfelt hug.

She had tears in her eyes when she said, "Welcome home, Dad."

"Now I've seen you again after all these months—"

"A year," she interjected.

"Year…when I see traffic stopped, I'll be thinking you're walking beside the road."

"Traffic will be just one of the problems you'll have to deal with." She glanced at Zane. "Sure you want to take on all these headaches? Mother included?"

"She getting along ok?"

Muir nodded—no need to ask whom he was referencing.

"Ask her yourself. She and Richardson have invited you and me to dinner at the El Tovar. On them."

"They must think a public servant's salary won't cover it."

"Prices aren't what they used to be, you know."

"Neither am I. But I'm gonna throw everything I have left into managing this Canyon. And if I can man up for that, I can handle a chowdown with your Mom and her real estate wonder. But let's get together one of these days real soon, just you and me. That is, if you can find time on your busy schedule."

Muir smiled. "I did this morning. And lucky me, I also tracked down a vandal."

Zane said, "Some use the word 'eco-raider.'"

She stared proverbial daggers at Zane, who took them like, he hoped, a dedicated eco-raider would.

Blake had neither acknowledged the backpacker nor brushed him off. The lean, hardened young man who strangely enough reminded him of himself in the days when he'd eaten fire for breakfast, had been waiting for five minutes, an eternity on his scale of patience, and now he angled in directly on their conversation .

"Really glad to have you running things, sir."

He held out his hand and Blake shook it without hesitation.

"Something tells me you're not a civilian, come here out of curiosity."

"You know, those chains you bolted to the Redwall—they're still in place."

Blake whistled.

"You managed to get down there? Or rather, up there on that cliff. Jiminy, I thought I was the last radical."

"Pioneer is more like it in my book. Activism with a capital A."

Blake smiled.

"Well son, that was a long time ago. I've learned the word 'compromise.'"

Muir added, acidly, "Mr. Bailey has quite a rep, Dad, but it's not for compromise. Rumor says he can hike you into the ground, cook scorpion stew, imitate a rattler, and trespass and damage private property."

"And likes to take the high road," Zane rejoindered. "You?"

"Whichever one you're not on."

Blake whistled.

"Looks like you two had a run-in that's still running. I imagine you're the Ranger on suspension, Zane. For punching one of our canyon tourists."

"Arsonist. He'd built a blazing bonfire and they were dancing around it like crazed clowns. Tossing their empties against a boulder, like they needed to see broken shards of glass littering the ground."

"Clarence told me they picked them up."

"Yes sir. After some unfriendly persuasion."

"You'd be referring to a fractured jaw."

"Yes sir. Got carried away."

"Which makes you a doubtful Ranger to deal with John Q. Public, drunk and crazed or not."

Zane didn't answer.

Muir said, "If there's anything to be said for him, and there isn't much, I know he did it in a cause he believed in. Mr. Bailey doesn't compromise on his principles. And I can't believe I'm saying this."

Zane stared at her, hostility giving way to astonished gratitude.

"I can't either," he said softly, "but I appreciate it."

"Support from the strangest places," Blake said. "Well Zane, come to my office tomorrow, around 7 if that's not too early for you. We'll go over your record and see if you're worth rehabilitating."

Muir cautioned, "He might be spending the night in jail, Dad." And then to Zane: "If nothing else you can take a shower while you're there. I don't want to see my father asphyxiated."

To this Zane just smiled, and shouldering his pack to head off, said to Blake Wilson: "Cuffs or not, I'll be there, sir." And to Muir: "You might want to cut those fangs. Might wound yourself one of these days."

And Muir to him: "See you at the sheriff's."

## Trouble Brews

The Grand Canyon lies off the beaten path of American freeways. To reach it by car, one has only a few options.

From the North, a state highway south of Zion and Bryce Canyon national parks branches down from Utah's Interstate 15 to the canyon's North Rim, but by comparison to the bustling South Rim, where visitation floods, here it can be said to trickle. Most travelers skirt the North Rim and head east and south, crossing the Colorado at historic Lee's Ferry and semi-circling the canyon in order to approach the South's main Grand Canyon Village.

Those who head down to the North Rim in summer will find visitors enough, and full lodges, but will not have to put up with crowds. Lines don't form for long at the lodge and its main restaurant, and elbows don't rub others on the few hiking trails along the rim.

The National Forest land here on the Kaibab Plateau is lush, wide and deep, and empty. Forest roads crisscross, but if one does not possess a good map, a full tank of gas can drain quickly in a confused coming and going.

In summer, that is. The North Rim is closed for most of the year by snow, including and especially all amenities, and welcomes only the occasional crosscountry skier or Triathlete training for extremes.

Or the occasional lost soul, by fate or design. To the northwest of this side of the great Canyon lies the Arizona Strip, a triangle of land that the few inhabitants know somewhat, but most everybody else in the wide American population not at all. It gives home to survivalists of every sort, and by rumor as well as proven fact, those self-styled freedom lovers who use their freedom to wink at certain customs and laws forbidden elsewhere.

The South Rim can be accessed from the South by an Interstate highway leading directly up from Tucson and Phoenix and Flagstaff, or Interstate 15 from California and Las Vegas.

But the principal access route is 40 East, whose illustrious forebear, Route 66, brought the motorized world to the Grand Canyon from virtually all points east.

East, Middle West, South and North, all motors arrive on I-40, carrying all and sundry. Most are welcome.

Some are not.

A few short days before some disrespectful trespasser marred Muir Wilson's company's billboard, a severely disrespectful individual was plowing fields at an Arkansas prison farm famed for its "no-nonsense methods" of inmate control. Danny G detested farm work, just as he detested most anything that didn't please him at any given moment.

Just now, frying in a springtime Arkansas sun along with other "detainees" under the armed supervision of guards, he was most displeased with guard Willie.

"Where you get that name, man? Real coon name, you know, went out with slavery. Which we're gonna bring back, sooner the better, so you can do this shit 'stead of somebody giving you a gun and pretending you got the brains to pull a trigger."

"Your bullshit's real thick today, Danny. Keep it up. I'd like real bad to put your sorry ass in solitary."

"Yeah, big man, show you're the boss. Put that gun up your ass and let's go at it, man on man."

"I would except you ain't no man. Whuppin' you'd be easier than spanking a baby. You'd be squealin' like a stuck pig."

"Yo mama, black boy."

"Take that shovel and get back to work. Sing one of your dumbass rap songs if it'll help your lazy ass."

"Hey," yelled over a white guard named Bobby, "let's lower the temps here."

Enraged, Danny G ignored this attempt at diplomacy and glared at Willie. "You wanna know something? Your black life don't matter." In a flash he scooped up some dirt in his shovel and thrust it at Willie's face and eyes. The guard choked, gasped, tried to clear his vision.

"Eat it, Willie boy," Danny sneered, smiling, enjoying the guard's discomfort.

Willie charged the prisoner and took him to the ground, punching at him furiously. Danny G's head snapped back. He yowled in pain—something Willie did had brought the hurt…

And just as fast as it began, the fight ended as the guard Bobby pulled Willie off his foe.

"Hey man"—meaning Willie—"what the hell you doing? You could lose your job for this."

Willie didn't answer, gasping with effort and anger.

Danny G said, "I coulda grabbed his gun and blown his head off. But I didn't. Rather have a broken arm than violate my record of good behavior."

He ended with a groan and grabbed his right arm.

"Don't look broke to me," Bobby said. "But we'll see what infirmary says."

"Bastard needs to go to solitary," Willie snarled. "Shithole where he belongs. Get up. Get up, you sorry excuse for a loser."

But Danny couldn't—or wouldn't. He held his arm, seemed in real pain.

"I'll take care of him. You get back to work," Bobby told Willie. "This ain't gonna go down so good."

Willie scowled, "For him, we need to bring back our famous electric telephone. Give him some volts he'll never forget. Not like you can get it up anyway, BOY."

"Jesus," Bobby said. "I'm getting out of here before you go down in flames."

Bobby gestured to another guard who now came up. "Watch this guy"—meaning Willie—"he's hotter'n my old lady on a Saturday night."

Bobby grabbed Danny's arm as gently as he could and hauled him to his feet

On the way to the Infirmary, Bobby pointed to a room where some prisoner-patients lay on beds, recuperating.

"Lucky them. They junk up with all kinds of shit our doc puts in their systems and get well with all the TLC we can give, which ain't nothing but feels like it. You, suffering like you are with pain that'd kill a horse, no such luck."

"He gonna give me some morphine? I'm dying here." The pained grimaces on his face intensified.

"Like we care."

He opened the door to a side room and gestured for Danny G to enter.

"We'll shoot you up with the proper opioids, don't worry."

Inside the room, an anteroom reserved for first responders, both men relaxed. Out of sight and earshot.

Bobby smiled. "My shift ends at 10 tonight. You reckon that little arm's good to go?"

"Hell, it could fall off and I'd go."

"You got the drill down? Overpower but don't incapacitate. I need to stay capacitated, know what I mean? I'll stick around till PTSD kicks in."

"You gonna join us?"

"Us? First you got to get out here. Lot of miles to go before you get to be a brother in arms. A real marshal, if you can walk the walk. Just 'cause I recruited you don't mean you can pass basic training."

"Hell, I been training all my life. I'll make it."

"Second, you got to get a car."

"Like I didn't grow up getting cars. And not a single one legal."

"We did a good job today. Recruited a patriot and put a African so-called American in deep shit. Which he won't get out of if I got anything to do with it. Hey, how is that arm, really?"

"Nothing I can't live with."

"Want a booster?"

"Whatever you got."

Bobby smiled, quickly rifled through medicine drawers till he found an appropriate vial.

"This oughta work."

He opened a plastic-wrapped syringe, juiced it up with the contents of the vial.

"What is it?" Danny G asked.

"How the hell should I know? Which arm?"

"Both."

# Going to Work

After the ceremony Blake Wilson walked with his team toward the main park office. They made for a sight not seen very often at the Canyon, where geography meant that the Ranger force was continually spread out.

Harvey Pine took the opportunity to brief his new superior on the contents of his evening's campfire program, which focused this night on "the Canyon squirels. Boy, it was hard to reduce my presentation to 30 minutes. There's just so much to say about those little critters, though some can be good-sized animals. I've seen one—"

"How ya doin'," Blake interrupted, asking a group piling out of a tourist bus. They looked like they'd been on the bus for a while, and the tour guide explained in excellent English, with an accent Blake recognized as French, that they'd come straight from Phoenix after a long plane ride from Paris.

"They could not wait," the guide said, bemused at her charges. "They work for La Poste, the French postal service, and they are excited just to see this place where they send so many letters."

"I'd have thought that meant New York."

"After," she said.

Blake often remarked how sometimes at the national park campgrounds, he could make the rounds and not hear a word of English. He himself in his time had picked up a lot of German, so much so that he wondered if he didn't have a working knowledge, enough to do quite well if one day he took the time to see Berlin and Munich and cruise down the Rhine. It was on his Bucket List.

"Well, welcome to our beautiful canyon," he said to the guide. "Appreciate your enthusiasm, and let us know if we can add to your enjoyment."

"Yes," one man said who was puzzling over his guide-book. He buttonholed Harvey. "What is this 'BC'? 81 BC?"

"Now that is some story. It's simple, but then again it's not so simple."

Blake hoped that Harvey would not run through 2000 years of world history in the Occident, but that remained to be seen, and anyway he had to get to the Office. He motioned to Josh and the others and they moved away as Harvey expounded.

Josh said, "He's as dedicated to his work as a cactus is to desert sand."

"Not as prickly, I hope."


It was still early and the Center's doors had not yet opened to the public. This meeting was being held impromptu in the Museum section of the Visitor Center. Tableaux of Grand Canyon geological strata loomed in the background all around and as he spoke, Blake circled, as if the mockup gave extra force to his orders on this, his first day on the job.

"You'll see on the duties board I haven't made any changes to Clarence's assignments. I want to see how things shake out and go from there. You all know the rules and the need for courtesy at all times in enforcing them. I will tell you this—people come here from around the world looking to see a natural wonder unparalleled where they come from. And my cardinal rule here's the same as everywhere I've been in our country's great national parks. Let's don't disappoint them. Give them an experience they'll remember for the rest of their lives. And always remember one thing. You might say it's the motto I live and work by: 'Don't block the view!'"

He waited a moment and then waded into their laughter:

"One more thing. Call me Blake. Now let's get to work!"

His rangers dispersed, passing Harvey who was just entering, looking a bit stressed to see them heading out so soon: "What did I miss?" he asked Josh.

"The riot act."

"Oh Lord. I need to know that act."

"It'll be posted on Facebook. Come on, let's get down to the business of running this park."

"But I'm always down to business. Mr. Wilson's got to know that."

"You want my opinion? He does."


Blake Wilson took a moment to eye his desk. Clarence had kindly cleared it of all odds and ends, but left a custom-made plaque that had been awarded to the Canyon ranger force way back when in the 1940s, carved delicately and amazingly from petrified wood, congratulating them for work well done and to come.

Years before, when he was newly married and "so wet behind the ears I needed a rain jacket," he'd seen this desk and thought it looked comfortable and sturdy and a desk he would never sit at, both from predilection—he preferred to be outside, boots-on as it were—and doubts he'd ever have the wisdom and experience to become head Ranger.

He definitely wasn't sure now, but here he was. Some Higher Up had been deluded enough to take a flyer on him.

He sat in the wide, comfortable leather chair. The back fitted his own, snugly and ergonomically he thought, but it remained to be seen as to whether his did. A lot of water had flowed under the bridge and down the Colorado since that first looksee many years ago.

More thoughts came rushing in, but he put them on the backburner. He had an appointment with his North Rim Rangers.

A few short minutes later Blake Wilson rolled up to the tarmac where the pilot and flight service owner Russ McGuiness waited by one of his rental helicopters. He was watching as nearby, one of his choppers finished loading a family of tourists who were bound for a flight over the Canyon's scenic viewpoints.

Blake got out and headed over immediately to Russ.

"Don't tell me I get the VIP treatment today, best pilot on the Rim?"

"Whoever that pilot is, he's wondering why you don't take the government chopper. You paying this out of your own pocket?"

"Plus tip. Got to save the company fleet for search and rescue. Call me dedicated or call me stupid, take your pick."

Russ smiled, held out a warm welcoming hand and shook Blake's.

"You ain't stupid, or at least you didn't use to be. Hell of a nice thing to see you back here, Blake. Been a long time coming for the Park Service to get its head out of its ass."

"And we wonder why they don't invite you to their Christmas parties. What keeps you in business, other than you've got the best flygirls and flyboys around?"

"Courtesy. Hell, I even gave them this group a discount, forget the reason why but it must have been a good one at the time."

"Well let's get to gettin'. I polished my speech, gonna do it a lot better for the North Rim crew."

"Why don't you take the wheel? Make you look like a rock star coming down for the fans and groupies."

"You'll do that for me?"

"They tell me you know how to fly these machines."

"Might be rusty though. Keep awake."

They got in the chopper, Russ waving to the tourist family as they took off.

Blake got into the pilot seat.

"How's business?"

"Booming. We're hoping the new boss doesn't rock the boat."

"He's no skipper, but he knows his way around canyons and machines like this one. It's a beauty, Russ."

"Mine. Bought it with my spare change, just for me and VIPs."

"Keep your fingers crossed."

He revved the motor and they lifted off. In seconds they left the Rim's terra firma and flew into the wide gap of sky between the Grand Canyon rims.

In a few short minutes of flight time through the drafts and wind gusts beginning to whistle as the new day advanced, they would arrive at the North Rim.

# Backcountry

Lucinda opened the Backcountry Office right on time at 8, and true to the tradition of backcountry hiking, a group of eager trekkers were already waiting—one could say, camping—outside the door.

Permits to hike the vast areas of the Grand Canyon where 99% or more of its yearly visitors never set foot or toe don't come easy. Not because there isn't room enough for them. Rather, as Lucinda liked to repeat whenever she drew Backcountry Office duty, "Backcountry in the national parks is a synonym for wilderness, and like the US Wilderness Act says, man comes as a visitor. He doesn't stay. And most of all, he doesn't stay in crowds.

"Crowds bring noise and pollution and before you know it, wilderness isn't wilderness any more. It's turned into a sidewalk. And we've got enough of those in the world, right? Whereas wilderness, well in my opinion we don't have nearly enough."

American tradition held that national parks should be open to everyone, but not trampled by everyone. So those who would trammel the Parks' wilderness had to tred carefully, "leaving no trace" as far as possible.

And though it wasn't possible to prevent anyone from encroaching on the parks' backcountry without permission—the US remained a land of the free—wilderness by definition took preparation and some sort of permission had to be required, and was.

"It's for you," Lucinda would patiently explain. "You get lost or have an accident, we'll know who you are, whether your car's still parked overdue in the lot, who to contact, and really, the basics we need to know before coming to your rescue."

"I'm just walkin' down for a Photo Op," said Freddie, a young man who in past decades would have been called portly, but now seemed lean and hungry. "Such is today's body mass," Lucinda liked to say, wincing as she did so. She entered every Iron Woman competition she had time for, and her own body mass reflected her dedication to flesh become iron insofar as possible. She was wont to run down the agonizingly steep South Kaibab trail and run back up in less time than it took for a couch potato to get up and fetch a beer. At least, this was her own sardonic description of her run time. Only Zane Bailey among the Park rangers could beat her, and rumor had it he was part deer, among other savage parts.

Nevertheless, Lucinda was nothing if not professional, and she never let her own personal preferences blotch her interactions with a less than iron General Public.

She told Freddie, "If you're just going for a stroll down one of the main corridor trails and not camping overnight, you don't need a permit. For dayhikes, all you've got to do is pick up your feet."

"I can do that. Kinda."

"We advise everyone not to push it. What goes down must come up, and the farther you go the hotter it gets. Take lots of water and don't overdo it. This is one park where less is more when you venture on the trails."

"I got a couple of cokes and my girl friend a Dr. Pepper. That'll do, won't it?"

"We advise cool clear water. Nothing beats it. Even Dr. Pepper."

"Okay, well..."

"Have a nice hike. And don't forget to read those trail signs, okay?"

Freddie headed off. Lucinda remarked that his lady friend to appearances also did not run in Iron Woman competitions.

She'd meant every word she said, as few days went by when some overly ambitious dayhiker did not go too far, too fast, with too little water. Dehydration killed a lot of people at the Canyon. Freedom to roam was a part of the national park experience, but all too often unthinking tourists paid more than an entrance fee for it. A fee not counted in dollars, but flesh and blood and, alas, life.

The next group of three men and women, all in their '30s, looked more fit, though the name proffered by the tallest, sporting a snazzy Stetson, suggested they might be carrying preparedness too far.

"'Joe Camper'?" Lucinda queried. "Something tells me that's a kind of pseudonym."

"Joe Camper" corrected immediately: "My friends call me that 'cause I've done a lot. Every weekend you could say. Real name is Eric Sims."

"Afraid we'll have to put that on your permit. All the other names legit?"

"Yep. 3 days, 3 nights."

Lucinda confirmed, "At the main corridor campgrounds. South Kaibab Trail to Phantom Ranch, up North Kaibab to Cottonwood Springs, then Havasupai Gardens on the way back via Bright Angel Trail."

"I'm kinda new to this," the to-the-looks-of-it youngest in the group said. "Not going to be that hard, no? I mean, I did some 5-mile training walks."

"You'd be..."

"Ray."

"Did you do those walks with a loaded pack?"

"No. Should I?"

"Joe Camper here didn't emphasize that?"

Eric/Joe said, "He's Cindy's partner"—indicating the blonde member of their group. "We just met."

"Well, that's what these kinds of trips can do, build friendships." She eyed Ray's pack, which he'd been conspicuously loading a few minutes before. "You didn't by chance bring along a kitchen sink, did you?"

Ray chuckled, without perhaps understanding the irony in Lucinda's remark.

"That sucker's pretty loaded," she clarified. "Sure you'll be able to handle it?"

"We're going downhill, aren't we?"

"In a pinch we'll just send him rolling down," Cindy jested.

Lucinda laughed along with them, but even though she worried they might have to do just that, she said, "Here are your permits. Please hook them to your packs. Have a good trip. Looks like it's going to get pretty hot today, so the sooner you get going…"

"Geronimo!" Ray said.

One of the darkhaired women in the group winced. "That is so uncool and incorrect. You better hope we don't run into a Native American Apache."

Lucinda added, "Or our Havasu ranger, Lily Dawnwind. She holds to traditions pretty hard. But last I saw, she wasn't carrying a bow and arrow."

Lucinda hoped they would get the point. They seemed like nice people, as most of the Grand Canyon hikers. It took some spunk to head off into the backcountry, carrying a heavy backpack, and amateurs or not, she felt they deserved a lot of credit. What they needed to learn, they would in the next three days. Ray would have a sore back and a lot more besides, but if he made it back up the trail—she'd foreborn pointing that out to him, that the Grand Canyon was mountain hiking in reverse—he'd stand corrected on a lot of reflex attitudes.

"Blarney gets bleached out right quick on these trails," she liked to say.

And up next: four gung-ho types with helmet cams and water bottles slung from necks and, she was sure just from the looks of them, packets of industrial-strength gorp.

"Jon Barzini, the Barzini party. Barzini like in the Godfather, you know."

"Right," Lucinda said, "pretty ambitious program you've got here. Down to the river, floating across, up and down and back. You know the Hermit is pretty tough."

"So are we," Mr. Barzini said, and the grins of his hiking mates chimed consent with the sentiment.

"Well for sure you'll get a workout," Lucinda said. "Just watch your step, one at a time, and watch those currents on the Colorado. We've got a search and rescue team here at the Canyon but you all aren't going to be easy to reach if there's a problem. Please don't break no legs."

While dispensing these cautions, which she hoped they'd remember, she was approving their permits. She handed them over.

"Won't be," one of Barzini's mates said confidently. "We've been training, Iron Man type of shit."

"Good deal. Wire these to your pack straps, and enjoy our beautiful canyon."

## An Old Pro

The South entrance to the Grand Canyon was manned—and that was a term whose accuracy nobody who knew him ever quibbled over—by Raymond Gunther. He was nearing 65, but retirement from the Ranger force wasn't an option he'd considered for one second, and tales were told that when he passed on, it would be standing up, in a Canyon entrance booth, hopefully after he'd just handed out for surely the millionth time (or at least umpteenth) the Park brochure, entrance fee receipt and the kind of have-a-good-day welcome chatter that many tried, but he'd perfected for almost forty years.

He'd become a Canyon institution, with newspapers calling him the "Grand Old Man" of the US Park Ranger force, though he grumped, "I may be grand all right, but don't call me old."

This day he'd gotten up at dawn, as per usual, done his strenuous routine of calisthenics and weights work that he liked to time with the dawn's early light, outside the cabin he'd built with his savings over many years. It didn't matter whether it rained, froze or fried, he was outside on his terrace, keeping his body much "fitter than a fiddle," he liked to say. To heavy snow he did make some concessions, preferring to postpone, but the snow had to come down in blizzard density.

He traveled a lot, but never to Europe or the Far East. He preferred to make the rounds of the country's great national parks. He'd never worked at any place but the Grand Canyon, however, and in this respect he differed from Blake Wilson. Their paths crossed on those trips, several times over the years, and they liked to recall how Raymond had given him tips and war stories when Blake joined the Ranger service and interned at the GC.

On one of their first after-hours rounds at the Canyon watering holes, he'd introduced Blake to Pat, his young, vibrant and lovely and very eligible friend. It hadn't worked out for Raymond with her—he was married to the Park Service, literally and truly—but he'd been happy and proud to see his friend succeed where he hadn't, and equally sad when the success turned to divorce.

For a brief while he'd been like an uncle to Muir. And though he wouldn't leave his beloved Canyon, it hurt when Blake moved on to one park after another across the USA.

That morning Raymond had finished his exercises, showered down and fixed a load of cowboy coffee. He knew Blake would stop by to say good morning before the ceremony, which he couldn't attend—"When duty calls, you can wait," he'd quipped when Blake arrived. "Anyway, I don't like speeches, even yours."

"Maybe because you've heard your own too often. Please tell me you've polished it after all these years."

"Nope. Just can't smile so wide any more. Teeth and gums gettin' old, you know."

"Hell, who's measuring?"

"You are, Big Boss. I'm proud of you. Must have listened to everything I taught you back in the days."

"Everything except about women. There I made a mistake. Or she did."

"Your mistake is in disremembering. I don't know the first thing about that subject."

"Makes two. We gonna have a beer once I find my way around? Lots more I need to learn. And this place is Priority Number 1."

"Rule #1. Watch your step at the Rim."

"That one I do remember."

"And watch your step, period."

"Gotcha. And my Rangers. Any bad eggs in the bunch?"

"Not yet. Or not that I can see. But I only see tourists coming in their cars and camper vans."

"Well don't let me keep you from your work. It wouldn't do to be late on my first day. Looks bad."

"If I am late, it'll be the first time in 40 years."

"Did I tell you?"

Raymond was already hurrying out. He turned slightly. Blake continued, "I found a good jewelry store in Gallup. Should I pick out a gold watch?"

"Not unless you need one yourself."

Sure enough, a camper van was the first vehicle to approach Raymond's entrance station this morning. Across the USA they sprouted like the tamarisk trees that were overtaking, and pushing out, the cottonwoods that had populated Western canyon streams for centuries.

"Morning. Welcome to the Grand Canyon," he said with the smile that seemed pretty wide enough to everyone who came across it.

"We are from Taiwan," the driver said.

"Happy to have you," Raymond said.

And he meant it.

# Campground

Harvey Pine liked campground duty almost as much as his campfire lectures, because he found multitudinous opportunities to teach and educate the temporary denizens of the splendid sites among towering magnificent pines.

"We don't have the Virgin River like they do in Zion," he liked to admit to those who'd come to the Grand after visiting that park with its towering white granite cliffs, green valley and of course, aforesaid river. This would come after said tourists responded to his small talk by recounting their itinerary, which often meant the grand "Circle Tour" that passed through Las Vegas, traversed Zion and Bryce Canyon National Parks, dipped down into Arizona and maybe detoured to Monument Valley, but inevitably ended here at the "greatest Canyon of them all."

"Of course," Harvey would say, "you can do the Circle Tour in reverse, but it just won't have the same exciting ending. Unless they reproduce the Grand Canyon in Vegas. They might. They've already got the Eiffel Tower there. Some folks ask me it it's real and I say Yes, but it doesn't speak French!"

And as to the Virgin River, he liked to say, "We do have a river here, but it's a lot farther down, except on the totem pole!"

Usually his laugh would resound the loudest at this quip, which he laid to the fact that it was more complex than most and required concentration and comprehension, and he never tired of criticizing the declining state of America's educational system—both public and private.

Harvey's duties at the campground were myriad, and ranged from collecting and verifying that the campground entrance fees had been duly paid, overseeing and sometimes doing-it-himself cleaning of the public toilets, the afore-mentioned chitchat with some of the campers—which he found worked better early, before they fell to the chore of packing up for the ride out to home or another destination—and miscellaneous.

Today he came upon a middle-aged couple from Spain who worriedly questioned him about the dashboard light that signaled an oil problem. But they'd checked and the dipstick showed full. So why the light?

"This is existential problem?" asked the husband.

Harvey checked and rechecked the oil level, soothed their worries with optimism as best he could, probed and analyzed the car motor.

Finally when he saw time passing and realized he was falling behind schedule—plus he'd found no solution—he said, "Yes, it's an existential problem. Nothing to do but keep on existing. Besides, it's a Japanese-made car."

"So, it is a cultural problem?" the tourist asked.

"You all have a real nice day," Harvey concluded, and moved on. He made a note to himself to use "existential problem" whenever necessary, i.e., when he came across a situation to which no ready solution existed, given the Canyon's diverse population, visitor use and overall entropy caused by both. The Rangers were there to manage and organize and deal with the chaos that was always liable to ensue, but some, like life, had no easy, quantifiable answer that made sense.

Like what he saw now. "Heavens to Betsy!"

Whoever had camped at Site 98 had left very very early, leaving some litter. But what was worse—cigarette butts.

Tears came to Harvey Pine's eyes. "They should know better. They DO know better."

That frustrated most of all. What were these people thinking? Lighting up in the middle of a pine campground that ranked very high on the Park Service's list of fabulous outdoor overnight sites (Virgin River or not). He was no Zane Bailey who reprimanded such dangerous pollution with a punch to the jaw. But he'd have given these folks a piece of his mind. He didn't use swear words, but after he was through, they might wish he had.

Harvey did some deep breathing, trying not to stare at the cigarette butts.

When he'd calmed down sufficiently, he picked up the waste material and moved swiftly toward one of the park trash bins.

"Conveniently and strategically located all around the campground," he'd say to campers—most of whom, thankfully, got the message. "There for all your pollution needs." This usually did get a laugh, but after this morning and those cigarette butts, he felt no desire whatsoever to joke about what always risked becoming an existential problem.

# Lawkeepers

Lincoln Williams relieved his colleague Sheri Franklin, who'd been handling the law enforcement command post for most of the night. The graveyard shift was usually rotated among the other members of the team, but the night had been exceptional with Blake Wilson's arrival and Sheri had volunteered to hold the fort while most of her colleagues attended the dawn welcoming ceremony.

"Real slow so far," Sheri said when Lincoln walked in. "Luckily. Didn't even have a complaint about some raven snatching a breakfast biscuit."

"That's the kind of nights and days we like. Back home in Detroit, we never have a slow night. Won't even talk about the days."

"That why you came West? Escape the inner city?"

"That and asthma."

"How'd the ceremony go?"

"Check it out on the Net. Missy filmed it."

"She include herself in it?"

"Hey, don't go there."

"I was testing. To see if you went there."

Sheri had met many tourists during her tenure at the Canyon, and one had made an extremely good impression on her. And when he kept leaving the campground to pester her with questions, and eventually resorted to desperate ones like 'Where do your prisoners camp?' she supposed that she might have made an impression too.

Luckily he lived in Albuquerque, which wasn't that long a weekend drive, but as time went on it got longer and as Sheri said, "so did our kisses."

So one day he'd popped the question and she'd said yes. All that remained were two big challenges, where to have the wedding and how to reconcile their respective careers without long weekend treks. They were getting there. Sheri loved her job, was good at it, and her fiancé Rick understood and respected that. Even though, as she realized, given park service transfers, "We might be bringing up a baby in the Sonora desert."

She was a first responder and member of the search and rescue team like Lincoln, and they formed the leadership of the 20 or so Rangers who made up the law enforcement team.

The phones and shortwave were beginning to buzz and the others were moving into action.

"Get some sleep," Lincoln told her, "and dream about a happy marriage, not your wedding shower. Which I am not confirming is going to happen."

Lincoln settled in behind his desk. He'd been surprised when he arrived at the Canyon and learned that Park Rangers enforced the law there. And that a dedicated team patrolled the length and breadth and above all, depth of the immense natural wonder. They specialized in EMT, fire control, search and rescue—you name it, they did it—not least answering questions about this and that as all the rangers did.

In short, they were not only Johnny (and Jane) on the spot, they were the sheriffs in town.

"I should have known," he told Clarence at the time, "but I guess I was concentrating on staying out of trouble. That was 24/24."

He'd been one of Detroit's most pugnacious youths up until the age of 13, on the street from dawn to dusk and often the next dawn, one of the several brothers and sisters abandoned by their father and to all intents and purposes, their mother. He'd never crossed over into outright and unambiguous lawbreaking, being that young, but he was on the cusp and when he'd been insulted once too often by a huge white kid who'd been doing it consistently and increasingly, he took a baseball bat and whacked his nose out of joint and not so far from taking off his head.

The kid took months to recover and amazingly, declined to press charges. Being nothing if not worldly wise, Lincoln saw the crossroads.

A court-appointed counselor reinforced that by saying, "You dodged a bullet, Lincoln, but the next one might have your name on it. 13 years old and your body lying in the street, bleeding to death. Maybe you don't think that's ever gonna happen and don't think it's real, like most kids. Come on then, lie down in the street for real one night. Feel the cold and rats."

So he did.

"I learned the value of a sleeping bag," he joked afterward. "But that sure as hell wasn't all."

He'd struggled up to 20 years old, then managed to get into a junior college, then survived a couple tours of duty in places he knew would never qualify as national parks—"too many bullets and Kalashnikovs."

Until he applied for the Park Service, he'd never visited a national park, and when to his great surprise he was selected and hired, he looked forward to it mostly for that very reason.

Except unlike tourists, he stayed, and the law enforcement bureau seemed to him ideal for his talents, such as they were, but mainly, knowing what constituted lawbreaking and how to confront and interact with those who indulged in it.

He was damn good at his job, and he settled in this day knowing that it would not be boring—it never was—but if they could get through it without an injury or lost or injured hiker, they'd have successfully managed another day in paradise.

# Grounding the Bird Man

Hiking at a rapid pace near the rim edge, Zane Bailey came up short: a Bird Man was facing him.

The creature--in actuality François, an earnest young Frenchman--wore a bright orange and blue hi-tech fiber suit. The elbows inflated outward, the sleeves ballooned with air, the whole resembled what it was, a one-man glider.

Only now the creature had a problem:

"Please, do me the zeep!" François implored.

"What?"

"The zeep, she is stuck."

"Ah..."

Zane understood and found the zipper in question, pulled it down...and ergo, François was able to begin getting out of his bird suit. Zane noted his bandaged shoulder.

"*Merci infiniment*," François said.

"You're François. The Frenchman that had to be scraped off Powell Butte last week."

"Yes, thee 'Bird Man.' I like this name, you know."

"Except birds don't crash on their butts. Don't tell me you're going to try to fly again?"

"Design flow, like zeeper. I'm fixing, you'll see, pretty soon I will fly like the *aigle*. Oh *putain*!"

He wrestled with the leg straps that theoretically, in Zane's non-engineered opinion, anchored the wings.

Zane cautioned, "You know, the wind currents in the Canyon, the lower you go the stronger and more unpredictable they get. They've brought down planes and helicopters—"

"No problem for Bird Man! I have studied this *meteo* weather."

"And if you happen to land in the river—even if you're all zeeped up--that water's so cold, hypothermia in five minutes."

"You Rangers, some job, eh? Always some crazy stupid *con* like me gives you worry. How you say when you jump? You know, the big Indian."

"Geronimo."

"Oh *putain*!"

This time it was a hole he'd spotted in the knee fabric.

"Has to be tight like the air you know. You see any other holes?"

A dubious Zane shook his head, smiled to allay the reproof:

"Maybe just one, in your head."

"Some day I market Bird Man suit. Then everybody can jump. You too."

"Let's put it this way. This canyon is a billion years old. Come another billion, I might." He shouldered his pack. "Watch those buttes."

Zane shook his head, gave him a last dubious look and hiked on, leaving François to his *putain* flying suit.

## The North Rim

When Blake Wilson touched down on the North Rim landing pad, Russ McGuiness complimented him.

"Smoothest ride on this chopper I've had since...the last time I flew it."

"Keep the motor running. Going to make this one short and sweet."

"Janey may have something to say about that."

Janey Ross was the tall Ranger at the supervisory head of the North Rim ranger contingent, and she'd prepared a welcome for her new boss not at any basic lookout post, but an area of exposed rock overlooking the canyon, a view if anything more spectacular than any comparable one at the South.

That at any rate was Janey's view, and Blake had been told, "She has views, if you know what I mean."

He'd heard other stories that gave him an image portrait of a Viking warrior, ready for battle 24/24 and capable of beheading her enemies. Which, he said wryly, "could make for a good supervisor."

So he was genuinely surprised when he saw someone who could well have passed for a svelte cocktail waitress. He instinctively knew well Janey would have reacted furiously if he told her this, so he kept his mouth shut. In any event she seized the first word.

"A little late. Been doing some sightseeing?"

"Well, when you've got sore eyes and the Canyon's right in front of 'em..." He held out his hand and she shook it firmly and swiftly.

"Janey Ross. We've got a busy day today. Like every day."

"Don't I know it. And I want to know more, a lot more."

They walked toward the waiting Rangers whom Janey had spared for a half hour or so from their daily duties to meet and greet their new boss. Blake had prepared a short speech similar to the one he'd just given, but tailored to the Rim where "seasonal" really meant something. The Rangers here alternated shifts with those on the South Rim but some preferred to stay put.

"I hear you're a faithful North Rimmer," Blake said to Janey.

"If you want to call it that."

"How would you call it?"

"Fewer crowds to step on my toes. I don't like getting stepped on. I kick back, you know."

"I also hear you take orders with a grain of salt."

"Clarence gave me a lot of rope. Haven't hanged myself yet."

"As long as it works, keep on till it doesn't. And that's what you might call my first order. Need any salt on it?"

Despite herself, Blake thought, Janey betrayed some pleasant surprise. He liked her frankness and no-nonsense demeanor. And if 10 minutes acquaintance counted for anything, he liked her, period.

"Mind if I give you a good introduction?" she asked.

They'd reached the waiting Rangers and Blake's sore eyes got a good gander at the view down into the natural wonder he'd always wondered at, no matter how many times he'd gazed into it. Today he thought it looked particularly magnificent and unparalleled.

"Make it to the point," he replied, "we've got a busy day."

He thought he drew a semblance of a smile from her.

# Trouble with a Capital G

"I don't like him."

"He is crazy and wild. There are some Americans like that."

"Yes, you find them in cowboy bars. He is the kind who will break his beer bottle in a fight and use this for a weapon. He scares me."

"You have seen too many movies. Look, he will take our picture and then we leave him."

"Please please Heinz, do not tell him we are going to Las Vegas. He will want to come with."

"Well, what do I tell him?"

Before Nadja could answer, a voice yelled from above:

"Y'all ready? It's showtime in the good ole USA!"

The subject of their fears and future plans stood on the Canyon rim, some 20 meters above where they had scrambled down to a ledge overlooking the great Canyon—their first glimpse of the natural wonder they had come from Austria to see.

He'd called himself Bill, joking "And that ain't Dollar Bill, 'cause I just spent my last one."

They'd met him in Tuba City where they'd stopped for burgers. Their Monument Valley weekend had been a dream come true, touring in their rental the immense colorful sandstone buttes and towers they'd seen in old Westerns. It was as if they'd reached back in time and entered the old Wild West of John Ford and John Wayne. They'd stayed at Goulding's Lodge and when recuperating from photos, sightseeing and hiking, lolled in the indoor pool before dining on huge beefsteaks and beer. Sure, maybe the cuisine didn't match their native dishes, and the coffee tasted like water to a couple raised on genuine Viennese brew, but all that went with the territory, and they were overjoyed to be passing their vacation in this territory. "Let's chow down on this grub!" Heinz chortled, and Nadja laughed even harder.

They adored the native fry bread they'd discovered on the trip, and they'd made a detour, retracing their route toward Utah and breakfasting at the diner in Mexican Hat. They'd found the fry bread there particularly delectable, very much worth a detour.

So it was later than they'd liked when they rolled into Tuba City. They fast-fooded lunch and ordered two huge cups of waterlogged coffee for the route. They were going to haul ass to the biggest canyon of them all, if you didn't count the planet Mars. They wanted to savor a few days on the Rim, gutbusting a hike or two down and back, then chowing down some more on chuckwagon steaks.

They'd been unable to reserve the campground. These days you had to pick your spot months in advance, and Heinz had dilly-dallied, to a verbal roasting from his wife. But he'd found an alternative scenario, one he assured Nadja would put them firmly among that community of cowboy range riders who took Land of the Free literally.

"Grand Canyon is big place," he told her. "We have tent, stove, flashlights, everything. I have made the calculation"— being an engineer by profession, he could do that with his eyes closed and didn't need software—"kilometers and kilometers of rim, and these Rangers, do they patrol at night? They do this so great job but they cannot be everywhere."

In short, they planned to park their car in a lot near an observation point and then hike to the rim far from any madding crowd and camp "at large—that means, where you want. This is home of the brave, you know, and we just, must be these brave."

Maybe that was why John found it easy to ingratiate himself with them and hitch a ride. He'd shambled up to them outside the diner—"Where he was?" Nadja asked, "behind some big rock? Poof, he was there. It was how you say, spooky."

"Don't exaggerate," Heinz said. He found John's brand of BS quite amusing and thought he fit his image of an unbridled American wanderer. He wouldn't cite a job—"Don't stress me with that shit," John smiled, "I'm living, know what I mean?"

He'd got right to the point.

"Y'all going to the Canyon? I'd sure appreciate a ride. My car went belly up and shop here says they can fix it, but you know how it is with these Injuns, they got their own notions and it ain't watch time. I mean, if I've got to wait a few days, I'd rather do it camping. Hell, my taxes paid for it. I got some dogs and we can do a wienie roast."

They'd been puzzled.

"Hell I can explain it for you but this old sun's beatin' down and if we hang around, those tubas are gonna start playing but we'll miss the sunset."

He'd hopped into the car with his backpack and large duffel and punctuated the drive west with commentary that Heinz and Nadja said had one central theme, despite digressions from here to there and everywhere: anger at liberals and communists who were threatening democracy in his beloved country.

"We have Communist Party in Austria," Heinz said.

"Very few people in country vote for them now," Nadja added. "They are like how you say, phantoms."

"They're there," John said, "like here, waiting to take over. We hang onto our guns, 'cause once they come out into the open, we'll be ready."

Nadja said to Heinz in her native language, "This is crazy stuff."

Heinz translated for John: "She says, this is so beautiful country."

"Wait till you see the big hole," John said. "Hey, let's head for the North Rim. You'll see the turnoff up ahead. That's where I'm going when I get my car back. Thinking of staying the winter, holed up somewhere in a dugout cabin gonna build with my own hands. North Rim's tranquil, you see. No crowds."

Heinz exchanged a look with his wife.

"Well," she said, "we have this plan."

John argued, "Well whatever the plan is, you can do it on the North Rim, that's what I'm betting. Come on, let's go."

He waited, and Nadja thought afterward that he was on the brink of forcing the issue in some way or another. She saw the turnoff just ahead. Turn right, they would head north toward the long lonely stretches of the North Rim. She'd read enough to know that there, they would see spectacular sights and magnificent sunsets. But an instinct told her they'd find fewer people, yes, and fewer resources, but less security if something happened to them.

Quickly she poured out to their rider their plan to camp surreptitiously on the South Rim. The turnoff came and went in mid-explanation as Heinz continued straight west. Nadja turned back just enough to see John smiling. For some reason she couldn't quite analyze, she felt relieved.

"Now that's what I call the frontier spirit. Suits old John here to a tall 'T.'"

Night was falling and they still hadn't arrived at the Grand Canyon when, providentially it seemed, they saw the Navajo Tribal Park turnoff.

"You folks got your itinerary," John said, "but take it from a cowboy, here you're gonna be free as a big old buzzard. I'll bet you a dime to one of your Viennese coffees they'll have headed off to their wigwams by now."

"Hogans," Nadja corrected. "On the Navajo nation they live in hogans."

"That what you call it, nation?"

Heinz added, "They have laws and a president and their own police. I read this."

"Well, their po-lice won't be patrolling this so-called park till tomorrow morning, late. They'll be hitting the whiskey real hard. I guarantee you they won't care if we camp on the land we let 'em call their 'nation.'"

Heinz and Nadja exchanged looks. And after a moment, "We have no reservation at campground," Heinz said to her.

She nodded and they turned off. John was right in that they drove free and clear past the entrance station that listed the fee as $10 but added the qualification, if this was too steep, any donations would suffice and be welcomed.

Nadja paid the full $10 fee and placed the bill in a lockbox provided for these occasions.

John shook his head and smirked, "You just financed Jim Beam."

"Who? I don't understand this."

"You will. Stay in this great country and you will."

John had showed them how to roast hot dogs over an open fire that he swore was permitted "on this here Navajo nation. Hell, how you think they made smoke signals? It's in their blood."

He roasted the dogs to perfection and to their taste, and Heinz and Nadja were content to "chow down" with their new acquaintance. They even tolerated the American mustard he insisted was absolutely essential to the experience, and which they found bitter and less tasty than their own back in Austria.

"It's part of the experience," Heinz shrugged.

John had borrowed one of the coat hangers they'd packed and unwound the wire. Both Austrians had to admit it made for an excellent skewer, holding several dogs at once and strong enough to endure the fire.

At dessert, plastic-rolled apple tarts the couple had bought at the Tuba City market and which Nadja remarked "might be tasty if they had any taste," Heinz joked, "Now you put it back together John, this wire."

"Hell no, you keep it in your backpack, folded up. Trick I learned a long time ago. Like I told you, out here in the West you wear a sweater in the morning and fry in the afternoon. That sun will whip your ass. And your car too. Why you've got to leave the windows cracked open. If your hi-tech keys fuck up—and they will fuck up—you can still jimmy your way in with this little home-made sucker."

They'd all learned that if you dallied in the evening and slept late in the morning, you missed God's own sunrise and that was a capital sin.

John placed a blanket that he said came from the Salvation Army, whatever that was, and rolled his sleeping bag over it.

"Don't believe in tents," he said. "I need to see starlight. You never know who might be sneaking up on you, know what I mean? Like the gunfighters."

"You are not afraid of snakes?" Nadja asked in all sincerity.

"I got more poison in my blood than they do theirs," John had laughed, and Nadja couldn't help but wonder if he was right somehow.

Nevertheless they followed his lead and didn't set up their tent. She was overwhelmed, almost tearful at the canopy of western stars that shined over them. She'd seen the heavens in full glory on their mountain trips in Europe, but something about the high desert here excited her. Later Heinz confessed he'd had the same sensations, as well as a powerful desire to make love to her. Why they didn't could have been laid to John nearby, who snored relentlessly. Heinz noted that other gunfighters would have no trouble tracking him down, night even more than day.

John had laid his bunk on the very edge of the Canyon rim. Nadja said to herself, when we are together again, Heinz and I, we will do the same. Though she for one wanted some kind of fail-safe system. She did not want to roll into those depths she could hardly sleep for dreaming about.

She did though, and woke at just the right moment. John was already awake, staring at both of them. Grim and unsmiling until she opened her eyes wider, so he could not miss seeing her awake. Then he smiled.

"Show's about to start," he said, meaning a Grand Canyon dawn. "Just got enough time for a quick coffee."

On this very early morning, as John had predicted, they had the place all to themselves. They were alone together in a West they could still call wild, if wild meant unstepped on by human feet for the better part of 365 days a year.

Heinz and Nadja hit the overlook for a wealth of photos. Their plan was to take each and every overlook on the Rim and record photos for their album. When they returned to Austria they meant to start on a large family, and Heinz' profession being hardly a conduit to wealth, they figured this might be their last chance to savor, hour by hour, the American West's natural wonders. Like thousands of tourists every day, they took pictures.

But unlike most of those thousands, and now that John had come along for the ride, they wanted to push the envelope a little. Heinz showed their newfound companion how to operate his expensive camera. "What do you call 'em, kroner? You musta shelled out a few for this sucker."

"Don't worry about cost. Take a lot. We do this once in life, you know."

"Hell, if you do fall it'll make a great pic."

Nadja hadn't appreciated this kind of humor, as with John in general, whose welcome was wearing out for her by the second. "We take him to village and goodbye forever," she whispered to Heinz as they scrambled down, very carefully, to a rocky outcrop below the overlook. In exchange for defying risk, they now had prime front row seats at the show. Clad in shorts and hiking boots, backpacks stuffed with water and gorp, they watched the splendid light and color of dawn, insouciant to the dangerous slope they'd come down.

Moved by the grandeur, the lovers exchanged a long, deeply felt kiss.

John was high enough above them to have to raise his voice, but they could still hear the CLICK as he took his first photo.

"Hell, I feel the heat up here. Give her another one, Heinz! Real wet and sloppy!"

"He is pig," Nadja spat to her boy friend.

"Is good advice though."

He leaned in and kissed Nadja again. Then again. They could hear the CLICKS from above.

"Pictures won't do justice to this," Heinz said, nuzzling his lover.

"Yes," Nadja giggled, "but if we have a child, he will see his parents have not much shame."

"Yes," he agreed, keeping on kissing.

Abruptly...a silence which didn't register at first. The lovers embraced as if it were the first day of the rest of their lives.

Or the last.

When Heinz reluctantly left off from his lover, he looked up toward the rim, wondering if John had changed positions for a better angle.

He didn't spot their erstwhile photographer. "He looks for a good vantage," he said.

"What is vantage?"

"Where he can get great photo."

But time went by and they did not see John. They exchanged looks, and had the same thought. Or apprehension.

"I will go see."

"And me?"

"I will come back quick. Enjoy the sunrise."

"Heinz—!"

But he was already scrambling upward.

He almost slipped--she let out a little gasp of alarm—but he regained footing, began scrambling up to the rim.

Nadja watched him climb—he was an experienced, outstanding mountaineer—and knew he'd leave her in the dust.

But as spectacular as this sunrise was proving to be, she did not intend to stay long. She decided to give Heinz five minutes. No more.

John had not trashed his hooked coat hanger last night after the barbecue because he intended to put it to use as he was doing now, deftly inserting it through the cracked window, dropping the loop around the  lock knob and twisting it to get a firm grip.

It took him hardly a minute, suggesting strongly that John, or Danny G as he liked to be called, had done this kind of thing before, maybe many times.

Once inside, he pulled out a pistol and slammed the car's ignition, exposing wires. He started fumbling with the wires, seeking a spark.

This too did not take long. The car roared to life.

Danny G began backing up...when the passenger door was suddenly jerked open.

Heinz jumped inside.

"What you do?"

"Steal your fucking car!" Danny G yelled, stunned by the foreigner's thick-headedness.

He spun the wheel around and shifted into Drive, but Heinz had grasped the situation immediately, despite Danny G's slur, and only hesitated in an effort to resolve the crisis amicably.

No longer possible, if it ever was, he began grappling with his now confirmed foe, who managed to wrench out his pistol.

Heinz grabbed it and with the other hand the wheel.

The car screeched into a spin, kicked up dust, and headed in a direction neither wanted as they fought fiercely for control--straight toward the rim.

Heinz and Danny G struggled frantically--

Nadja had gotten to her feet and headed up. She heard the sound of a car—coming her way, and the Canyon's.

The car approached the abyss--

Danny G managed to free his pistol from Heinz' grip and slammed the Austrian's hand on the steering wheel with the butt.

Heinz's hands slipped off--

Danny G wrenched the wheel around.

Tires turned at the literal edge of the rim, scuffling dirt over the very edge.

Heinz grabbed again—

Danny G slammed Heinz's head with the pistol—

The car lurched—

Below the rim, Nadja's eyes widened in shock as a body came tumbling down past her--Heinz--and hurtled over the ledge beside her toward the depths of the canyon...

And just after—the car, tumbling sideways.

Nadja screamed.

Heinz grabbed rocks, hung by his fingers—but let go to lurch aside and avoid the falling car.

He just managed.

The automobile bounced once, crushing rock and sending up a cloud of gravel and sand, then tumbled into the void that was the great canyon. The sound of its impacts on the cliffs reverberated for a long time, the time for Nadja to jump down toward Heinz.

He had slid further down and just before falling after the car, had grasped and held rock while his legs dangled over the cliff edge. Blood flowed from his head wound.

Nadja saw him as the dust rose and sight cleared. She scrambled down further, almost falling herself.

She reached down toward him.

"No," he gasped, "I will bring you down..."

"Take my hand!"

He hesitated, then reached up slowly...

Their fingers touched, gripped--and loosened--
Heinz slipped out of her grasp, fell into the abyss—
Nadja's desperate scream echoed far and wide, all across
the Canyon in the early dawn.

## Search and Rescue

Lincoln Williams was managing two growing and ever-present concerns at the Canyon: litter and search and rescue. The former kept piling up as it were, despite a more ecologically conscious breed of tourists and locals.

"Numbers, that's what we're up against. Population. The more people, the more debris."

Lily Dawnwind had stopped by to pass the time. Rumor had it that she and Lincoln were becoming more than colleagues, but no one had pinned either of them down yet. The Canyon was a big place and had many discreet sites for discreet lovemaking—not to mention, great views when the more casual lovers tore their eyes away from each other.

"That's because people don't adopt the Native way. Love and protect the Earth because she is our mother, and you don't throw garbage on your mother."

"I like the Native way," he said with a smile, which together with the sentiment coud be taken as rife with subtext.

Problem #2 had to do with how to allocate Rangers, interns and perhaps some volunteers to patrol the much-used Canyon main trails for the summer, when temps became dangerously, fatally hot and unthinking hikers pushed their envelopes way too far and way too fast. Search and rescue on the trail took too much personnel power and often exhausted the Ranger rescue team, so stationing Rangers up and down the trails insofar as possible helped warn and educate the balladeers to risks. "A few ounces of prevention," Lincoln  liked to say. "Does wonders."

"They'll still do crazy stuff," Lily cautioned.

"You headed down to the Village?" he asked.

"Yeah, in the heat. Want to come along in case I exceed my limits?"

Lincoln looked around at his colleagues. They were all busy, on the phone or otherwise, but out of easy earshot.

He said in a low voice, "Yeah, might be exciting to see you exceed your limits."

Likewise her, low voice: "I'd slap the hell out of you but I know it wouldn't do any good. You'd be the same bad boy you've always been."

"I'm reformo."

"Yeah, and I've got some swampland in the desert to sell you."

A call came in on the fixed line reserved for emergencies. Lincoln took it, listened for a moment. Hung up, got up.

"Tribal Park. Hiker's gone over the Rim."

"Breathing?"

"They don't know. Want another pair of eyes."

"You watch your step now. Know your limits, ok?"

"You do the same."

"You got my number. Don't forget it."

"As if," he said on his way hurrying out the door.


Muir Wilson had a busy day ahead, full of rendezvous with prospective buyers, and the first one at 10 am looked to be the most important, or lucrative, depending on one's perspective, and hers had moved inexorably toward the latter since her parents' divorce and her taking her mother's side in the painful separation from her husband.

There hadn't been Defcon-style rancor, but her mother's unhappiness at changing homes to out-of-the-way, remote or just plain wilderness parks had gotten to her psyche. To Muir's, less so. She'd enjoyed the changes of scenery and most of all the scenery, had grown up to be a bookish tomboy and not found that an oxymoron, but she felt her mother's pain intensely.

Her relationship with her father suffered, deteriorated, then all but vanished as the years went by and he went from one stationing to another, always putting out metaphorical and sometimes real fires. He was the Fixit Ranger and never settled down to one place like Raymond. The Park Service needed his kind of foolproof organization, efficiency and people-friendly management.

None of which worked in his marriage.

Her mother had opted finally for security, stability and prosperity, and Muir, who'd almost grown up on wild hickory and pine nuts, came to like more and more creature comforts. Knowing the downside of such, she found she made for an outstanding salesperson of civilized fruits like deluxe condos and sleek heated swimming pools, preferably with Jacuzzi.

She felt "damn confident," she texted her boss and father-in-law, about the "10 zero zero," as this couple had made it plain they'd "made their money," a phrase which she knew always meant, they'd made enough to fill Uncle Scrooge's Money Bin and now just needed a place to fix hot toddies and watch the sunset.

She had the place, and by 10 the offending graffiti would have been scrubbed or painted over.

In the meantime, and before her commercial business, she meant to make damn sure the perp got on a City of Tusayan police docket.


Officers Jimmy Deer and Louis Rainer, Jr., listened and took copious notes as she detailed the trespassing, property defacement and other assorted misdemeanors she charged the felon with.

"Alleged felon," Jimmy corrected.

"Like there's any doubt. You know this guy, right?"

The officers exchanged looks that verged on admission.

"Met him once or twice," Louis confessed.

Muir could read their looks and tone. She stared hard at them with a transparent look of her own.

"At the Shortbranch Bar. You know it?" Louis asked.

"I do not." This said curtly.

"Tusayan's chic hangout, you might say. We did encounter this individual and we do know his reputation as a…well…"

Louis searched for words and Jimmy helped him out.

"Individualistic individual. If you know what I mean."

"I do. That's why I'm here. To <u>file charges</u> against this individualistic individual."

"Right," Jimmy said, and turned hastily to his complaint form, but before he got very far the individual in question walked in.

"Hey guys," he said in a tone of jovial familiarity.

Jimmy and Louis looked embarrassed.

"Please take a seat, sir," Louis said sharply. "You're under investigation."

Zane did, across from the complainant, Muir. The daggers she was staring at him sharpened. He had changed his T-shirt from earlier. This one looked new and never worn from its well-folded, bright white.

The cops stared at the slogan.

"Stenciled it myself. What do you think, guys?"

It read, "SUPPORT YOUR LOCAL ECO-RAIDER."

"I think it's prima facie evidence," Jimmy said.

"I think it's more evidence you're an asshole," Muir snarled at Zane.

"We know you don't share my convictions," Zane retorted, "but namecalling won't get you very far."

"I don't want to get you far. Jail cell's right over there."

Jimmy pulled out a blotter.

"Well, let's get down to the alleged facts of this affair. Did you take pictures of the damage to your property?" he asked Muir.

"Many," Muir answered. "If you'll dust the billboard for prints, you'll find his all over. Kind of like bird doo-doo, you know."

"This is why I came to the party, guys," Zane said to Jimmy and Louis. "She spits out insults like melon seeds, except she's twenty times less tasty."

Muir barked, "Like you know what that taste is. Not in this universe, mister. Or any other worth living in."

"See what I mean," Zane marveled.

"Uh," Louis interjected, "time's slipsliding away, folks."

But Muir had more. "I filled Chief Wilson's ear with facts —not alleged—about you. And if I were you, assuming you can make bail which I doubt you will, I wouldn't bother coming to that meeting tomorrow. Waste of time. His, I mean."

Louis' cell rang and he picked up, listened. Handed the phone over to Zane.

"Blake Wilson," he said, "sounds bigtime urgent."

Zane smiled, loving Muir's comeuppance. "Hope I won't waste his time."

But what he heard wiped the smile away right quick.

Josh Allen greeted Navajo Nation officer Frank Stone without the usual good cheer and camaraderie. He knew him well enough to know his Navajo name, but this was business and he'd called because Josh doubled on the Search and Rescue team and they needed not backup, but very special first responders.

"How far down is he?" Josh asked.

"If we knew that, you wouldn't be here," Frank Stone said.

Standing nearby was Nadja, sobbing, just this side of hysteria. Josh moved over to her, put his arm around her shoulder, trying to comfort her.

"Nadja...show me where he went down."

With trembling arm she managed to point to the spot on the precipice where Heinz fell.

Josh nodded to the officers, then stepped over the rim, scrambled down the shale slope and scree and didn't stop till the very edge of the precipice, a frightening exposure.

He didn't expect to see Heinz and in truth, rehearsed in his mind how he was going to tell Nadja that her lover and fiancé had fallen to his death and she would have the horrendous task of identifying his mutilated body.

If it could be recovered, perhaps piece by piece.

He'd done it before, for fallen hikers, and despite his experience and trials by fire, never found words to comfort. Perhaps because he wasn't sure such comfort existed. He was an anomaly among what was left of his family in that he found no consolation in religion. He'd resolved to live his life to the full, and though he had become a conscientious, one could say outstanding civil servant and Ranger, he'd been known to tie one or two on throughout the night if he got lucky with an amorous tourist looking for a fun evening.

Last night he had, and the evening had stretched toward Monday morning. He hadn't expected to count on his long range vision this day, but here he was, and he wasn't about to make any concessions to vertigo.

Still wondering what he was going to say to Nadja, he inched closer, to the very edge of the rim, and looked with a hope he worried was futile.

But there, way down, maybe a quarter mile down, he thought he saw movement that didn't equate with a vulture or squirrel or any other canyon animal.

At first he saw just the multi-layers of geological history

Josh pulled out his binoculars, put them up to his eyes, adjusted the focus--

Saw Heinz.

Still alive, face and hands bloody as he clinged to the rim of another dropoff. Trying to keep from slipping off, his heels dug into the dirt and rock.

He wouldn't be able to hold that perch for very long, and Josh doubted that the man for this job could make it in time to attempt what would be one hell of a hairy rescue. Assuming it could be done.

One would have to be half crazy to even try it.

Providentially, he knew just such a man and he knew he'd go for it.

He turned and hauled ass upward toward the rim.


Blake Wilson pressed plenty of flesh after his speech to his North Rim troops, and he could have gone on, getting to know this part of his Ranger team assigned to the wild, alpine-forested area of the park whose facilities opened to tourists only a few months per year and was still pocketed with snow from a wet winter.

But when Janey said, "I'll walk you to your chopper," he got the picture. He liked her bluntness and directness. Future Head Ranger material, he said to himself, but not directly to her. Not yet. Let me get through my first day at least, he thought.

"Prep for opening going ok?" he asked.

"We're ready and willing. No late season storm comes through, next Monday it is."

"Good. We've got a lot of reservations. What about the trails?"

"Still a lot of snow. I'd prefer we discourage the gung-ho types for another week or two."

"If they're gung-ho, they won't be too discouraged."

"That's a fact. But I'll give it a shot."

"Something tells me they'll feel the pellet."

His cell rang. Blake listened a moment, then said to his caller, "He's not official. He'd have to volunteer. Think he'll do that?…right. His number's still on the list. I'm on it.

"And clear a space for my chopper."

Janey surmised the situation quickly as they neared the helicopter and Blake waved to Russ to start the motor. "I'll be goddamned if I'm going to lose a civilian my first day on the job."

"Get it done, Blake."

He noted that he liked her moral support, and the tone and way she phrased it.


Muir was driving fast, about twice as fast as she would have liked on the Grand Canyon main road east, leading out of the park.

"Faster!" Zane Bailey shouted.

He'd not even hung up and handed back Officer Louis' phone before she'd grabbed her car keys and headed for the door.

"Haul ass!" she yelled at Zane.

Seconds later as they ran toward her 4x4 and he just managed to catch up to her—no easy feat, as he knew she ran marathons—at the door, he asked, "How did you know—"

"If they asked for you it has to be a really desperate situation."

And as they got into their seats and she revved the motor and screeched off, buckling up on the run as it were, she added, "like you."

"East, Nation park."

Now, en route, Zane was one unhappy passenger.

"Faster!" he yelled again.

"Traffic!" she yelled back. "I'll pass when I can."

"Pull over!" he demanded, "pull over!"

She gave him a WTF look.

"I'll take care of your precious car."

And a scant moment later, he was roaring down the same road, in the same vehicle but passing willy-nilly and at what her adrenalin reserves calculated as warp speed.

"Learned this in Italy," he said as he moved left to pass and the oncoming cars swerved off pavement to avoid crashing into him.

"I've been to Italy," she said, "saw lots of bouquets at roadside."

"Just go with it," he said, just managing not to clip a terrified camper van that gave him as much space as it could—an inch or so, she thought.

"As if I don't have to," she managed to gasp out.

Quicker than any sane person would have said possible, they were racing into the parking lot where Heinz's car had been, then on foot across pine needles and leaves and rough ground to where Josh Allen, joined now by Lincoln Williams, was waiting with the terrified Nadja and Frank.

Zane hurried to buckle on the harness his colleagues held high and waiting for him.

"Hairy?" Zane asked.

"To the max," Lincoln answered. Then, glancing to see that Nadja couldn't hear: "Can't say he's still there. Fingertips." Josh intervened, "We're all you got—Search and Rescue's full up on the South Kaibab and Bright Angel."

"Count me in," Frank said. "I can hold a rope."

Zane smiled. "I know you can, Frank. I've seen you do rodeos."

Josh said, looking apprehensive, 'You know, being suspended from the force and all, you don't have to—. "

"Like they say," Zane said wryly, "it's my funeral."

And with that, harness buckled, walkie-talkie slung around his neck, he leaped back over the rim. He was just able to hear Muir yelling, "Bring him back!"

Zane virtually ran down to the small ledge where Heinz rested, Josh and Lincoln having all they could do to retain control of the belay rope.

He took as much care as he could, given his speed, to not kick up too much debris. The shower of rock and dust, insignificant on flat land, became a menace when impelled by gravity. Pebbles could tumble down and hit Heinz with enough force to injure and break his grip.

And as Zane went over the first cliff edge, he saw that Heinz not only had a feeble hold on the cliff rock, his feet had scarcely enough room to rest on the thin ledge where he'd managed to stop his fall.

Zane marveled that he'd been able to hold on this long.

"Hang in there, big guy. Help's arriving."

Heinz said, his voice hoarse and raspy and weak, "Please hurry!"

Zane did. In a moment he'd reached level with Heinz.

He began walking vertically sideways toward him.

"Muscle up," he said in his walkie-talkie.

Up above, Lincoln and Josh did. Josh nodded toward Frank, and he moved over quickly to take hold of the rope.

Heinz almost sobbed with relief when Zane approached.

But he panicked. He grabbed at him, groping for his rope line.

"He's panicking!" Zane radioed.

Lincoln: "Don't let him take you down, man."

But he did.

Heinz lost footing and fell, floating out into air toward doom...except Zane grabbed him, saving him from the depths below and certain death.

For as long, that is, as the rope handlers could hold.

Zane held onto him for their dear lives as their feet dangled over 3000 feet of empty space.

And dropped down...

Heinz freaked, seeing the void below...

Zane used everything he had to hold him fast, knowing it was a losing battle if his handlers didn't pull him up—and quick.

"Pull!" Zane yelled.

But Lincoln and Josh and Frank were being dragged toward the edge by the weight of the two men—they struggled to regain control as feet scraped on the dirt ground and they edged toward the cliff.

They strained, Lincoln shouted, but they couldn't hold the slippage.

Until a pair of hands came to their aid...Muir's.

She grabbed the last section of rope trailing behind them.

His intervention made all the difference. The three men and one strong woman held the rope firm, no slippage.

"Pull!" Zane yelled again, "we're floating!"

Slowly, all muscles straining hard, Lincoln and his reinforced team began pulling hard, hauling the two people below back up.

Zane was using all his strength to hold Heinz against his body.

"Step up!"

With a combination of shoving and pushing, pulled up by the rope from above, he managed to get Heinz back onto the ledge where he was before.

Zane announced into the walkie-talkie: "The Eagle has landed. Relax."

"How the hell can we do that?" Lincoln radioed back. "No more rope-a-dope, okay?"

"What's your name?" Zane asked the Austrian.

Heinz gasped it out. He was trembling, in tears.

Zane began to unhook the belay.

"Heinz, listen, give me 10 seconds. Like they say, don't move a muscle. Can you do that?"

Heinz was breathing hard, and barely—but he managed a nod.

"Good. Now we're going to cross dress. As it were. And don't tell anyone I used that term."

He buckled the harness around Heinz' waist.

"But...how you keep from falling?"

"Super glue on my toes. Where you from?"

"Austria."

"Always wanted to visit Vienna."

"I wish I was there now." He looked down, still shaken and aghast at what he saw awaited a fall. "My God."

"I don't blame you. I can't stand heights either. You're locked in. Hold tight to the rope and you'll see your lover in five. Or ten max."

Heinz was trembling with shock and fear but managed to blurt, "This will make me so happy!" He was almost sobbing.

Zane announced into the walkie-talkie.

"Okay fellas, take him up!"

Up above, the three men and Muir started hauling Heinz up.

"'Fellas,' he said," Muir groused, pulling hard. "Sexist pig."

Heinz gasped a little as the rope tightened taut and he had to step off the ledge. But immediately he felt reassured as the rope held and he was hauled up toward safety and salvation.

"Thank you."

Zane smiled. "Just doing my job. Don't forget to admire the scenery. It's once in a lifetime, and I'm thinking you'll have a long one."

As Heinz headed up safely toward the rim, Zane managed to turn—literally, on a dime—a nickel would have been too wide—and look down at the scenery below. Nothing to do now but wait, so he admired the magnificent view.


When Heinz arrived on the rim, it took just a second for Lincoln to unbuckle him.

Nadja embraced him with a bear hug and kisses.

Lincoln radioed, "Made it! Ok, sending it down. Come back to Mama."

They let the rope down. The handlers watched it slide down and then over the cliff below.

"You got an eyeball?" Lincoln asked.

There was no response. They kept lowering the rope and harness.

"Now?"

No response.

"Now?"

Ditto.

"Zane? Zane? Come in, guy. Talk to me."

Still no answer.

In the emergency of the moment, they had hardly heard the roar of a helicopter landing behind them.

Lincoln looked back at Josh, Frank and Muir, trying not to look worried.

Blake Wilson stepped forward, indicated to Lincoln who handed him the walkie-talkie.

"Zane, this is Blake Wilson here. Can you hear us, man?"

When there was again no answer, Blake said peremptorily to the others, "I'm going down."

They hesitated. It was the Boss, after all.

Muir soothed: "He's never seen a mountain he couldn't climb."

Moments later Blake had strapped on harness.

He looked at Muir. No one had thought to ask her feelings, but he was her father. She read his look.

She said, "He's not done insulting me in this life. He's down there somewhere."

Blake nodded and let himself down.

The rope haulers belayed him down, and when he passed out of their sight, they only had the walkie-talkie to cut the suspense.

"See anything?" Lincoln asked.

After a moment, Blake responded: "If this is the ledge in question, he's not on it."

This hit his colleagues and Muir hard, but they all maintained composure.

"Going lower," Blake radioed, and they let out line. After a few moments, Blake said, "Got a view to the Esplanade."

Suspense.

"Movement." They all listened up. "He's on his way to check out the car. Free climbing. Lord God almighty, that is one hairy cliff he's tackling. Can't say for his chances. Where was he when they gave out good sense? Holy hell, that was some maneuver. I think the boy's going to make it."

During the reportage, Muir had been getting angrier and more frustrated by the second. Worry had turned to fury at having to worry.

"If he does, tell him to go fuck himself!" And then to the others: "You guys can handle this. I'm going back to work."`

And then a final fillip: "And after 'go fuck yourself,' tell him I'm going to make a big sale!"

# Back to Work

When Blake Wilson pulled, climbed and shimmied his way back up to the Rim with the help of his rope handlers, he found Heinz and Nadja virtually cemented together, as if they wouldn't want or manage to separate any time this decade. But much as he admired true love in the flesh, he focused on brass tacks.

"Why isn't this man in the hospital? Blake asked.

Josh answered, "He's got some scrapes and contusions but physically, he'll come out fine. Of course the shock is something else."

The effort made him grimace, but Heinz managed to rail, "He was maniac!"

Blake asked, "Can you give us a description?"

"In Austria, I am painter. If you want, I draw him, this maniac!"

"We want," Blake confirmed. "After a doctor's care and a good night's sleep. The hospital can arrange an extra bed for Nadja."

And then to his Rangers.

"No rest for the weary, gentlemen. Let's move these folks to some creature comforts."

"I heard you were a man who didn't leave witnesses. Seems like I put too much trust in reputation."

"Say something like that to my face, you may think different."

Danny G stood on the very edge of the South Rim. His newly acquired iPhone was working well and he didn't really need to check the network from a spot that overlooked the deep deep millenia-old crevasse below, but he had to make sure the phone functioned this time. He'd picked it from a purse. The unlucky Japanese tourist had no doubt noticed very soon that it had been a mistake to react so viscerally to the Canyon and leave, what's more, the amazing photo op to her husband. But she had to watch over her brood of three superactive children who risked any minute to challenge the iron safety barrier stobbed into the canyon granite.

"I admire her maternal instincts," Danny G thought, and were it not for him grabbing her phone, he'd have said so. As well as, "Put these kids on Ritalin."

But no. He'd contented himself with the phone. A flunky had answered, and would have given him a quick sendoff except his name rang a bell and Danny wasn't the type of caller who could be put off by a flunky gatekeeper.

His correspondent came on the phone and they got down to business.

"You're a noisy man," Marshall Hood said. "And I don't mean that in a good way."

"Hey, shit happens, you know. You'da sent me some transportation I'd be getting baptized right now, so to speak. Had to hitch with some drunk Navajo thought I was the Great Spirit."

"Listen up, Great Spirit. My men—and my women too, they'll hand your ass to you right quick—my troops got to earn their transportation and room and board and every other privilege we can afford. Hear what I'm saying? These so-called Park Service law officers couldn't locate an acorn if it hit them on the head, but you're sticking out like a big old oak tree."

Danny G let this sink in for a long moment, then got down to some iron tacks.

"Could be I put too much trust in your reputation. The people I've talked to say you mean business, real patriot-like, but I'm not hearing that. I'm hearing a guy looking for excuses not to take on a serious recruit. Put me up against one of your boys and let's see who's still standing. I guarantee you I won't be kissing dirt."

"Tell you what. You go off stealing another car, you're gonna bump right into a roadblock or exit station, get your ass caught in a sling and lead them right to me, and if that happens, I will personally cuff you and turn you in to law enforcement. With all my blessings."

"I'll tell you what, you people need me in a big way, like big. I can handle any bad shit comes your way. You want proof? They say you know this Canyon. So give me an exit ramp won't have everybody and his retarded little sister tramping along. I'll walk out, and when I do, I want one of your big-ass SUVs waiting for me."

Marshall Hood listened. He wasn't used to talkback, but it told him something about Danny G that he was pleased to hear.

"I'll give you an itinerary. Call it an obstacle course. Call it a trial by fire. Call it whatever the hell you want. Don't think you can make it. But if you do, open arms. You make it to the Rim, we may even send you some transportation."

Danny G listened up. The "itinerary" involved more than a walk in the park. But he'd been a survivalist and had gutchecked himself more than once. He did add, "Send a woman to fetch me. After all I'm gonna go through, I'll need to relax."

"I'll believe you when she sees you."

Then he concluded: "I'll say this—if you make it, I'll have some open arms waiting for you. We need patriots ready to go the last mile to keep this country great."

When he signed off, Danny G noted that dozens of frantic calls had been made to this number, trying to track down the phone and on the delusional assumption he might answer and out of his heart's kindness, return it to owner.

Right. Anyway he thought, they're all in Japanese. You'd think that on a visit to this great country, they'd take the time to learn some English. But that's Japs for you. Foreigners, immigrants. This country was made for real Americans, and people like him and Marshall Hood were going to fight to keep it that way.

Lily Dawnwind had left the morning's ceremony and headed toward Hualapai Hilltop. It was a long ride on the Interstate, then turnoff for over 60 miles across plateau country to the parking lot which overlooked Havasu Canyon and her village. Lily had grown up there and had no desire to leave, though she'd been tempted when she reached adolescence. A great wide world beckoned outside the canyon and its high cliffs and blue-green waters of Havasu Creek, and she'd been able to do some traveling.

But no matter where she went, she felt the ancestral and spiritual bonds holding her firm and hard, and after all was said and done, she didn't want to break them.

So when a pause in work and duty happened, as now, she went back to her village. This time instead of her usual foot trek she'd arranged to hitch a ride on the mule train that was carrying a load of tourists.

She arrived just in time, greeted her friend Samson the drover, then headed down. She'd checked in with her colleagues and learned about the various search and rescues undertaken on this busy day.

She was puzzled by the Austrian tourist episode. Glad it had ended apparently without loss of life, but a car going over the Rim and into the canyon did not happen every day, thankfully, and she regretted that the Canyon would have to be blighted by the hulk of a burnt-out car.

Given the situation, she suspected her R&R might be short lived, so when she reached home she greeted her mother warmly but took off right away for Havasu Falls. Like many who lived in the village, she accepted Havasu Creek and its wonders as part of the scenery and left the falls to the tourists who poured in in increasing numbers every year.

But today she joined the half-dozen or so who were enjoying a swim. She plunged in and swam over to the waterfall. It was always hot in the canyon before one reached the village oasis created by Havasu Creek, and now she relished the cool waters and spectacular falls. She dove under the cascade and spent some time under, watching the curtain of lucent water shining in the sun. Soon the light would change as the earth turned and the high cliffs shaded the Creek all afternoon.

Time passed so very swiftly, and before she went back to the hectic rush and sometimes hysteria of daily human doings, she wanted to slow it down as best she could, there in the beautiful waters.

Zane Bailey had made it down to the cliffside where the rental car had lodged and burnt. "To a lot of crisps," Zane thought. It had scrunched against a boulder, if not for which, gravity and momentum might have carried it much further down. As it was, Zane saw little possibility of it being recuperated. It might stay down here like the Titanic, for almost a century. A rusted hulk degenerating slowly, but never completely, in the winds and sometimes rains but mostly, desert heat.

Knowing its fate, Zane edged closer on what he thought from eyeballing was the most perilous section of his improvised jaunt. He had one goal in mind—see if the remains of a driver lurked behind the wheel.

Slowly, slipping sometimes in the steep earth of the cliff-side, he made his way to the carcass, which was still smoking, the drifts whirling every which way on every gust of the daily winds that swept the Canyon each morning as the hours passed. Given their force already, he knew they would be whistling soon. When he reached the car, he leaned in close, nostrils flaring against the stench of the black metal corpse.

The front door had shut and remained firmly closed, whether on its descent or before, he could not say. Heinz could. But what Zane did know was that no body had been cindered behind that wheel, no matter how fierce the fire.

Maybe the driver had fallen out of the car and the door slammed shut on the way down.

But he had not spotted a body on the way down. He would check carefully and hard as he made his way down to the Escalante route and the trail that would take him to the Tanner Trail and his exit route back up to the South Rim.

He hoped Heinz would be able to gather himself together from the shock and tell a coherent story. Given Zane's knowledge of rescue trauma, that would not be right away.

He turned away from the car. He had a little water, about 90% less than he should have to be tackling the trek ahead of him. Even this springtime, temps would be pretty damn hot until he got closer to the Rim. He'd have to be careful. But then again, if he'd been careful, he wouldn't have gotten to this point where most sane people would have not dared to tred.

"One step after another," was what he counseled hikers, "starting with the first." Advice understandable by a five-year old child.

He started with his first.

Muir Wilson had arrived at her company's building site just in time to welcome Alice and Brian, a middle-aged couple who looked much too young to retire.

"We're looking for a view," Brian emphasized. "Going to be working from home. My business is built up and humming right along. All I've got to do is hit the 'Enter' key from time to time."

"He convinced me," Alice said. "God's country, that's what he said."

Muir smiled. "Well, I like to say, if God could take a holiday from watching over us, he'd sure like to live around here, 'cause he did some A-1 masterful creation."

"That's beautiful," Alice said. "Did you get it out of a book?"

Muir's smile widened. "Got it from a former friend. Kind of a hippie type. Lost in space, you know, not of this earth. Social services have him on their radar."

She noticed the maintenance workers they'd hired on short notice scrubbing away at the graffiti. Luckily the soap obscured what was left of radical commentary.

"Shall we move on? We've got a great duplex I'm sure is going to interest you folks."

## JoeBlevins Dotcom

It had been a long first day, and it wasn't over yet. Blake Wilson looked up from his desk because he scented odors of perspiration that could only come, at the Grand Canyon, from a hiker who'd earned his arrival at the Rim after buckets of sweat had been poured off a hardworking body, to blend seamlessly and almost instantly into trail dust.

Surprisingly however, this particular hiker, though emanating scents that did not originate in Chanel #5, looked dried. In fact he was, and he read Blake's question before it was asked:

"Spent some time under the hand dryers at the lodge toilets. They work good. You know, half the time half the air's wasted. People take off with wet palms."

"Or in your case, since I'm supposing you were monopolizing one whole blow dryer, really wet. And since you deprived John Q. Public of one of our convenience facilities, tell me if it was worth it."

"No cadaver. Whoever our perp was and what he was doing here besides hijacking a car, remains to be seen. HE remains to be seen."

"We're waiting till Heinz is cleared for a full interrogation. Doctor says he was more shook up than he thought. Delayed shock reaction. Anything salvageable from the car?"

"Cinders."

Blake nodded. "Good work on the rescue. But you took chances. You always take chances from what I've heard. I can lift your suspension and I will, because you deserve another chance. One condition though, and for you, I've got a feeling it'll stick in your gullet like a cholla thorn."

"Since I could eat a horse right now, I'll take it."

"For now you'll be doing grunt work on trails, cleaning and reinforcing. Nothing involving interacting with the general public. Someone leaves some TP on the South Kaibab, you put it in your garbage bag and move on."

"Can't even give them a tongue lashing?"

"Think of this as a probation period. Tie your tongue to your pack and leave it like that."

"And this probation period lasts…"

"Until I say finito. Take it or leave it."

Blake reached into his desk drawer, pulled out a lavender-wrapped bar of soap, plopped it on the desk.

"From my daughter, in the event you survived."

"Do I look like a guy who'd use lavender-scented soap?"

"You might think of it as a poisoned pill. She was pretty angry with you."

"Nothing new."

"From what I know of her—and I should know a lot more than I do, I am so sorry to say—most men she doesn't give a second thought to. Doesn't want to waste her time. You get a second thought. That's a step."

"If I want to take it."

"At least take the soap. And by the way. Use it."


Zane Bailey liked to use the public showers at the Grand Canyon because they provided a true democratic experience for all those who hadn't rented a hotel room or arrived in a well-equipped camper van or, as in some cases, those who couldn't be bothered to scrub down after a gnarly hike and preferred to head home lickety split.

He however liked to wash down the grit and grime while listening to a myriad of languages in what was really one big communal locker room—sans lockers.

He'd picked up quite a few phrases of French this way, and just now he was working on his German, as clearly a busload of tourists had seized this occasion after a long ride to the Rim. He thought he heard the word "*bier*" batted back and forth, and that seemed like a good idea after a long and event-chocked day, and he could tell from the shadows scrimmed by the steaming hot water from his shower that the sun was setting.

In truth he preferred dawns to sunsets. The supernal beauty and variety of the latter at the Grand Canyon always amazed him, but melancholy followed. At time passing, at the darkness that would shroud all the canyon wonders, at the woman's love that would not shepherd him through it till next day's dawn.

"*Bier*."

He was on probation, and that he could get through in a song, but he knew already that Chief Wilson was a perspicacious individual and deep down, doubted seriously that once reinstated, Zane could toe the line and temper his rebellious ways in order to get reinstated. In other words, suck up to authority and promise to never again beat the hell out of a careless, arrogant asshole hiker liable to put the whole Canyon ablaze with his forbidden campfire.

"Not very likely," he thought. "I wonder if science has come up with some anti-kiss-ass pills I could take. (pause) Not that I ever would."

He recognized that his fellow humans were, after all, part of the environment. "For better or worse, and in my view, mostly worse."

As he was toweling off a man behind him said, in a non-German accent, "Hey pardner, spare that nice blue soap a couple minutes? Left mine at the campsite and I'm too whipped to go back and fetch it."

Zane turned and saw a typical tourist, American for sure, backpack slung over his shoulder, wearing shorts whose make he didn't recognize.

The American read his look: "Yeah, dumb ass, that's what I am, and a dirty one at that. But I'm ready to clean up my act, manner of speaking you know."

"Well, if you don't mind smelling like a lily flower." He tossed him the soap. "Gift from a lady."

Danny G took a whiff of the soap. It wasn't hard to whiff.

"She don't like you too much?"

"Neither dirty nor clean, but she believes in generosity. Keep it."

"Any port in a storm, they say. But this one's a one-off. I'll give it to these Krauts."

"Germans."

"If you say so. Hey, I owe you one. Soap I mean."

"Not lavender."

Zane moved away as the tourist moved quickly into the shower and set the water running.

"Which site you at?" Zane asked, raising his voice.

"You want a dinner invite? Sorry man, my lady and I got business, if you know what I mean."

"Yeah."

He didn't know why suddenly he'd asked the question about the campsite. The answer forthcame without hesitation, which he didn't think was so likely from a man on the run, a man who'd sent Heinz to his likely death that morning.

Everyone was on his radar now. After all, he'd come back from suspension, and the job of Grand Canyon National Park Ranger started now.

Missy explained politely to the Canyon tourist, who looked freshly scrubbed and smelled of lavender and either habitually spoke so softly and self-effacingly she had to concentrate to hear, or else had a reason not to look or sound conspicuous, that mule train rides were booked long in advance and unless there was a cancellation, he had no chance of finding a spot for tomorrow morning.

"So what do I got to do, hang around all day and pray?"

"Well, some people do that," she smiled. "Sorry, these trips have become so popular. People are like loving this canyon to death."

Danny G had to catch himself from adding, "Like I'd like to do with you, baby," but he was smart enough to know this would burn himself into her memory, and he sure as hell didn't want that. So he just murmured, "Really disappointed. Wanted to see that Colorado River. Been waiting all my life."

He hoped humility and desire might bring a special dispensation, but no. And in any case, some joker behind him, he now realized, was filming him on his cellphone.

The joker butted in, "Me too, and let me tell you sir, if you can't wait a year like I did, catch my YouTube post. JoeBlevins Dotcom. Every step that mule takes, I'm doing a commentary, like I did at Yellowstone."

He swiveled the lens to Missy.

"Joe Blevins. Here to check in."

"Yes sir," she said, after a quick checkoff on her list, "you're good to go."

Danny G knew Joe hadn't noticed his first reaction to his being filmed, but he couldn't be sure the camera hadn't caught it.

He lingered, and walked out with Joe.

"Yes sir, you are one lucky man. When can I catch your video?"

"Gonna put it up soon as I get back. I've got 300 plus followers already. Gonna sit outside my tent and edit. You at

Mather campsite? Come over and watch, give me your input. 'Course I've got final cut."

He laughed at his own joke and Danny smiled along with him.

"Hey, how about I film you heading back to your tent? You know, like a different perspective."

"Don't expect any money or credit now. This is an auteur film. Joe Blevins producer and director."

"And principal actor. Hey, don't be modest. We're just changing the camera angle a little bit. I mean, being an auteur and all, you know how directors go from close shots to medium shots."

Among his other failed attempts to learn a lawful métier, and meet his own unrealistic expectations regarding his singing talents, Danny G had studied some film terms. Some vocabulary had stuck in his head, but that was all. He was a wannabe in every way except lawbreaking now, which he'd become quite good at. From experience, he knew Joe B hadn't a clue, and would bite at the bait.

"Yeah, hey, I was going to propose that but didn't want to impose, you know? You've probably got all kinds of shit to do."

"I'm on vacation, Joe. Really glad to help. So when do we call 'Action'?"

"Like right now. We'll get a good look at the campground and my home away from home. That's what I call it, my home away from home."

"Brilliant."

He took Joe's iPhone.

"Already set and ready to go," Joe said.

"Perfect."

And for Danny G, it was.

# El Tovar

Ordinarily Zane Bailey avoided the El Tovar "dining experience," which was best suited in his mind for tourists and local folk who craved a night out at something other than your basic burger and fries restaurant.

Of course, this opinion was not at all founded and buttressed on the fact that he couldn't afford the menu, and even if he could, the fact of paying such money for a steak he could buy on sale at the Canyon market and grill over his camp stove offended his sense of environmental sustainability. "You can sustain the world on a hell of a lot less than snob prices paid by snobs who'll shit it all out just like any other person on the planet. Except it'll go out with the crap sauce they served, crap in more ways than one."

This unnuanced statement was said to none other than Muir Wilson, on their first date. And last to date, possibly till the end of time, as it turned out.

It was also the last time he'd set foot in the El Tovar bar lounge, and why he did it this night he couldn't quite say. He did like the Navajo nachos, which were just barely affordable on his current non-salary, and the pretty damn tasty local craft beer. Plus the lounge looked out onto the Canyon, and tonight he'd felt like melding civilization with the wilds that he loved so much.

Maybe, he thought, I'm thinking about Heinz and how he came so close today to never experiencing this natural wonder, with the woman he loved. Death would have robbed him of both. He hoped Heinz was getting his vim and energy back, and that tomorrow he'd be afoot and raring to go.

He, Zane Bailey would be, but as for the woman to love...

He ordered a beer and savored it, gobbling the nuts and chips that the bar, being classy or wanting to continue to be, offered to every customer, even those shuffling in from the trail.

When he thought of those myriad trails into and alongside the Canyon, he remembered the first time he'd hiked the Hartley. He'd been on a spree, vowing to rush up and down each Canyon trail in one day, a practice almost universally discouraged and which he never failed to emphasize even to the most experienced and Ironmen hikers. But which he ignored in his own case. More than once he came close to dehydration and, in a word, death. But he prevailed. Somehow.

The Hartley was known as one of the most difficult on either Rim, but also spectacular, and he saved it for last. And to savor it completely, he broke up the hike into two days, planning to camp for the night at Panorama Point.

He wanted solitude and expected it, the Hartley not exactly being your well-traveled highway. Sure enough, when he arrived at trailhead, nothing stood in his way but fear itself, and he didn't feel any fear.

He started down, reveling in the silence, the smells of pinyon and juniper, the occasional Canyon squirrel or chipmunk, the ubiquitous pinyon and juniper, and above all, the splendors opening up to his grateful eyes as he descended.

This day he set a more gradual pace, but still he was surprised when he heard bootsteps behind him. He picked up his pace, but they came closer.

He stepped to the side of the trail, a narrow place not for those fearful of heights and exposure. He couldn't stanch the curiosity over who was tailgating him, as it were—disdaining a certain kind of trail etiquette in a rush to trek and slowpokes be damned.

Later he confessed to her, "If my eyes had been sore you'd have been most welcome, but you were crowding me."

"You were blocking my view. Trail etiquette says, you stand aside and let faster hikers pass."

What he didn't say to her, then or later, was that she was so knockout attractive to his eyes, sore or not, that he had trouble fashioning sentences.

Later he realized he'd seen her before, a few years ago when he'd hired out for the summer as a rafting guide on the Green River in Utah. He was driving an ancient school bus of boaters down to their put-in at Mineral Canyon. The dirt road, blasted out of the cliffside, was no highway in the sky, and it took his concentration to keep the bus on its not-straight but very narrow and precipitous descent.

Midway down one of his rafting company's competitors, in a van much more comfortable and modern, had halted because of a boulder fall. He could see the driver motion to his colleague, and she hopped out of the van to deal with the boulder.

Zane put the gear in park and made ready to hop out himself and give her a hand—the boulder was just that, a heavy beast indeed—but the woman, who seemed still to be a quite young girl, seized the boulder without hesitation and half pushed, half-lifted it out of the way to roadside.

Zane heard a spontaneous "Whooo" from his passengers, an astonished gasp of disbelief and admiration at her strength. Shared by him.

At the river he'd only seen her in passing, downriver where the other company was helping their clients load up canoes, but she'd made an impression.

Now she was doing that again, on the Hartley Trail.

"After you," he'd said, "ladies first."

He expected some kind of repartee—trail etiquette and all—but all he got was, "Careful not to kick up debris." And moved on.

"Wouldn't think of it," he said to her back.

Here too he thought his quip called for a response, but if it came, it was lost in the wind.

In no time she had turned a corner and passed out of view.

He thought for a moment about speeding up, but she'd made a crack that meant, don't pull up the rear behind me, keep your distance.

So as much as he'd have liked to admire the view of her, aesthetically speaking, to go along with the Canyon, he did not hurry and didn't see her again.

Until he arrived at Panorama Point.


Muir had played rugby in high school and felt she could handle herself very well with or against men, and had done both in her past, which was filled with several of what used to be called "admirers."

She got along very well with the opposite sex and told her mother and stepfather, when they dared ask about her personal life, that men made up a significant part of the human species and so had to be taken into account.

"That's not much of an endorsement, honey," her mother said wryly.

"Well, most of them don't deserve endorsements." She said it matter-of-factly, not pejoratively, as most men factually and through no fault of their own did not live up to her talents and accomplishments. She'd been a straight-A student and top athlete, with the aforementioned rugby only one of the sports she excelled at.

She went to Vassar, despite her biological father's concerns over "elitism," and her stepfather's pride over same. And she could have landed in New York, as a highpowered exec with an MBA in hand—and maybe she would still get one, though as a Magna Cum Laude with unbeatable recs she hardly needed it.

But she'd come back home, such as home had ever been during much of her peripatetic childhood before the divorce. Why? She asked her diary, which she penned almost every day of her life and in truth, served as her only real confidante.

"Maybe it's the West," she wrote once. "In my veins and heart and whatever soul I've got. Some of the parks we lived at made me thrill, but when we came back to the West, it set my heart and soul on fire and helped me forget my mother's unhappiness for so many years."

Then she added: "Maybe I came back for her."

And "But not forever."

Muir had set up her camp and settled in at Panorama Point when the man who'd eaten some of her traildust lolled in. One day she would find out that he'd been expelled from numerous schools for inattention and other, more serious lapses. "Did you ever crack a book?" she asked.

"Lots. The ones I wanted to crack. Like the collected works of Bob Dylan. You can listen and read at the same time. Did you know he won the Nobel Prize?"

Muir had wanted solitude on her hike—one reason she'd chosen the difficult, isolated Hartley Trail. She'd soon be starting a job for her stepfather as chief salesperson, and she'd wanted a carefree dose of wilderness and nature before embarking on a 9 to 5 plus.

But this guy looked like he was settling in too.

"You don't have too far to go to the river," she said. "It's beautiful down there."

"Sounds like you've been there, done that. Why stop here?"

"Maybe you haven't noticed this magnificent view."

"You're blocking part of it."

She considered that rude. He was in great shape but on first acquaintance, she thought that he lacked breeding and perhaps, the right qualities from the neck up.

"You need a permit to camp here. Like mine."

She nodded at it, wound around a cord on her pack. His did not have same.

"Yeah? Well see, I'm training to be a Ranger and we haven't got to that part yet. Thanks. You know the rules and we applaud that. Want to dine together? I've got some great freeze-dried beef stew."

"I'm going solo this trip."

And at every one where you're the campsite neighbor, she came close to saying. For his arrogance. But just because of same, she thought it might be water off a duck's back.

She found him attractive in a certain way, if only because he didn't seem intimidated by her. Or hid it very well.

She turned away and busied herself with her camp prep, conspicuously hauling out her camp stove. He got the hint and strolled to the edge of the dropoff from Panorama Point. He pulled out a mattress and sleeping bag that looked as if it had been used by the US Army at some point not long after D-Day. He sat and settled into a Zenlike meditative pose.

She'd done plenty of yoga and could recognize an amateur when she saw one, a pretender who thought he might impress her with his close rapport to Nature. That was a mark against his perception, that he found her so superficial she could be Zenned into his sleeping bag.

As the thought passed, he turned and said, "Sunset's better over here."

"I'll keep that in mind."

But when it came, in even more than the usual splendor this evening, she chose a spot across the Point, on a crag that took some doing to get to. She'd been surprised before and after, when she scrambled down, once almost losing her grip, that he hadn't offered advice or made any comment about how hairy the climb to the rock viewpoint was. Most men would have freaked when they saw what she was doing, where and how.

She knew he'd noticed her, and from time to time looked her way. But not a proverbial peep. Suddenly the erstwhile seducer had become the Quiet Man.

When she got back to her campsite, she launched small-talk at his back.

"Some sunset, eh? Why I love the Hartley."

He turned, proving that he hadn't suddenly become transformed into petrified rock.

"You lost viewing time playing eagle."

"I do free climbs."

"You lost viewing time on that boulder move. Lot easier technique than that one."

"I didn't say I was some kind of pro."

"You didn't have to. It was obvious."

"So why didn't you stop me? For my health and safety, Mr. Maybe Future Ranger?"

"Enough platform down below to break your fall. 80% chance anyway. And me not being a Ranger yet and having read your body language, I figured I'd better let you expend some of your smart ass scrambling around that boulder."

"You didn't expend yours, that's clear as that sunset. Only not so nice."

"Sorry. Still in training, you know."

"Have a nice evening."

Only that wasn't that. In the waning light of evening she wrestled with her camp stove and glanced from the corners of her eyes at the freeze-dried vegetarian meal she'd carefully and meticulously chosen from the best and reliable organic providers and feared it would have to remain in plastic.

Much against her druthers, she walked over to where her Panorama Point neighbor was preparing his own meal.

"Any ideas how I can get this thing to light?"

"Have you tried matches?"

Ignoring the wise ass aspect of the comment, she said, "I've resourced every possibility I can think of, but considering you think differently from me…"

"Well, let's see what Mr. Bizarro can do."

He studied her stove carefully…

"It works by induction…the plaque should warm up."

"Except it doesn't."

"Bingo. You've understood the problem. Sun's gone down so we can't resort to solar power. The solution rests in our hands."

He fiddled around with the stove for about fifteen minutes, turning it upside down, sideways, in short, every which way but loose—correction, he also loosened the plaque and peered inside.

After the said fifteen minutes, she realized:

"You don't have a clue what to do. The only thing you haven't tried is juggling it."

"Good idea."

Her look told him all he needed to know about what she thought of that good idea.

"Mine's old-fashioned but it works fine. Be a shame not to enjoy that hummus stuff you brought along. At the very least you can see if it's edible."

"The one and only reason I accept your proposition, despite the sarcasm, is to honor the organic growers who worked hard to produce it, with minimal impact on our environment."

This gave him some pause. Then:

"Bravo. Please, be my guest."

A storm hit that night. Muir thought she had never seen such a lightning show. They sat on Panorama's rim and watched it as if they were at the cinema. Some drops hit them from time to time, but the storm was battering the North Rim with ferocity and sending rain in sheets and waves down toward the Colorado. Sometimes the thunder drowned out their conversation, which had fallen into a mutual detente mode.

About midway through the storm Muir noted, "I don't know your name, and you don't know mine."

"Details."

A boom of thunder—and it truly was that, so loud it seemed to shake the canyon cliffs—interrupted, and when it finally rolled away...

"You don't look like a 'Joe,'" she said, "that's too ordinary. And whatever you are, you aren't ordinary, I don't think."

"That's what people tell me. They say, 'Zane, what weird shit have you done lately?'"

"The only Zane I ever heard of wrote Westerns."

"Bingo. My Dad loved them. That was about the only thing he loved. Not my mother or me. Maybe he's still alive somewhere."

"My father is somewhere. He's been a lot of somewheres. National parks. I think he had a choice of naming me 'Canyon' or 'Muir.' In those days my mother went along with what he wanted. One day she didn't, but the name stuck and I like it."

"'Canyon.' Great name. But you can't go wrong with 'Muir.'"

"Spoken like him."

Once their IDs had been established, they went off into a conversation about the West and conserving it. She realized that he was, in the truest and sincerest sense, a True Believer in conservation, safeguarding and protecting the planet and battling those who denied that it needed saving.

She was as well, but selling real estate at the Grand Canyon, she felt quite sure, did not fall into his range of approved activities.

Not that she needed his approval. On the other hand, he'd lent her the use of his camp stove and he'd make a decent companion for the hike to the river tomorrow. Not that she needed a companion.

"I admire women who have the fortitude to hike alone into the wilderness," he said at one point, adding, "assuming they've got enough smarts to know the dangers."

"Right," she said, "bimbos like nothing better than to lug a 40-pound back into the middle of nowhere with not a Sugar Daddy in sight."

"Touché."

He looked out over the canyon darkness.

"You want to know my one regret?"

She didn't answer. "Well, I'll tell you anyway. It's that I have to sleep. I'd like to enjoy this 24/24."

Adding: "With the occasional human being for company."

"Lucky him. Or her. The occasional lottery winner. I on the other hand am crawling into my bag for a good night's sleep. Going to watch the dawnrise."

"Don't tell me you're tired. We've only done half the Hartley."

"I ran a marathon this morning. In Flagstaff. You weren't there, no?"

"Busy crocheting. Well look, if you'd like a companion in that bag…"

"Only got room for a scorpion. It's less of a pain. And I'm not at all surprised you'd beat your head against a wall when you knew you'd be beating your head against a wall."

"Ouch. Hey, I had to try. Good night then. Sweet dreams and all that."

"Don't fall off that edge."

"If I do, stove's all yours."


So they laid themselves to rest, Zane waiting till midnight before reluctantly deciding he needed a few hours for the challenge next day. He enjoyed listening to the sounds of her breathing in her sleep. She did not snore, and he felt sure if she did, the sound might not rival a harp, but it would please his ears and he would enjoy the music.

The next day after a divine sunrise where they managed to remain civil to each other, maybe even at times grateful to each other for sharing it together, they hiked down the Hartley. Muir turned off at the Tonto, heading toward the Hermit Trail and the hike out.

"Happy hiking," he told her. "How about a drink tonight at the El Tovar? My treat."

"Looks like you're heading down to the river. And let me say, yesterday you didn't break any speed records. You really think you can hike down and back up and have the energy to drink a beer tonight?"

"Depends on the kayak."

He explained that he had an inflatable and planned to cross the Colorado, explore the trail on the other side, then cross back.

She listened incredulously.

"Do me a favor, ok? Take a selfie on the river crossing."

"You don't think I'll have my hands full?"

"So much that when they fish you out at Lake Mead, I'll have a pic to remember you by. You're not even half crazy. You're full-on crazy."

"Is that why they call me Insane Zane?"

"I'll give you some motivation though. I'll hang at the To-var bar till 8. If you do manage to survive, or better, give up your loony itinerary, I'll treat for the beer."

"Deal. See you there, cowgirl."

As he zipped down the Hartley, she thought: What a fool this mortal be, one of those extreme sports kind of guys who ended up plastered on a cliff wall after freefalling and chan-cing upon the wrong downdraft, leaving their loved one or ones to pick up whatever pieces could be found, much less picked up. Not a guy for her.

She would go to the El Tovar because she also could do some business there, but this cowboy sure as hell wouldn't make the date. And if he did, it'd mean he'd run into a trail-side dropping of common sense and done an about face. As-cending the Hartley even from Panorama Point was no pic-nic.

She wondered if he'd ever done the Hartley. He hadn't said. He'd moved fast down the trail, much faster than yes-terday. But that didn't mean he could do all he wanted to do in one day.

Insane indeed. Well, RIP. She turned toward the East on the Tonto.

Now, at the bar at the El Tovar, Zane smiled, remembering how he'd managed to put a look of astonishment on her face which she hadn't succeeded in hiding when he sauntered in at

5 minutes before her deadline of 8. He'd even had time to shower down and look fairly presentable.

They'd had some fun over the beers, him showing the photos he'd been able to take despite the "river crossings from hell," and her admiring his fortitude despite herself.

"Don't ask me to follow you into hell," she warned, however.

"Just cool the beer for when I get back. Too hot there for brews."

She did pay, and not for just one, and as they felt good, she proposed a dinner at the El Tovar. He agreed, wanting to spend more time with her, and hid his panic. The Tovar menu didn't cater to the down and out with minimal bank accounts. She got the picture when he ordered a grilled cheese sandwich which of course, wasn't on the menu and was only prepared at Christmas, for charity purposes.

She recognized him as a certain charity case at this point in his life, and would have sympathized except that the discussion unluckily swerved toward finances and her job, beginning tomorrow.

After he'd accused her of selling out, betraying the Grand Canyon by perching a subdivision on the Rim, going to bed with Mammon—all this a very polite and Bowdlerized version of what he actually said—their relationship ended before it really began, and the phrase "mutual recriminations" didn't describe the half of it.

They skipped dessert.


Zane shook his head, remembering that catastrophic dinner, after which they could never bump into each other without bumping heads.

Pity, he thought as he dug into his pocket for the coins to pay for his beer this time—eureka, just enough—because he still found her attractive despite her heinous ideas and go-dawful proposed despoliation of the Canyon.

Even more attractive now, speaking of the devil, as she was coming toward him on high heels and a springtime dress that in his opinion, flattered to the max a figure that didn't need flattering.

"I'd like to be the bear you're loaded for," he said.

"You used the soap. Thank God. You're being invited to dinner."

"I note you used the passive voice."

"We all want to thank you for the rescue today. A 4-square meal. Which I kind of think you haven't had for some time?"

"Like maybe, ever."

"Think about it though. You won't like some of the company, and I'm not talking about me. If you want my opinion, my father wants some backup."

"Proud to be his backup. Just don't expect me to behave well."

"As if..."

Blake Wilson made the introductions as they took seats around a table he had made sure to reserve himself, one of the best with a view out over the Canyon.

Zane thought it looked particularly lovely this evening, golds everywhere and the light sharp as could be against the buttes and cliffs, the trees which had found an aerial home by taking root where it seemed none could, in the rock, swaying green and soft in a light wind at sunset.

Unfortunately, he thought, this gloaming couldn't be shared with Muir in peace and silence and shared appreciation. He would have to deal with those all too numerous, in his view—though one would have been too numerous for him, it had to be said—who thought only of transforming it with concrete and swimming pools.

"Pat and Richardson Stark," Blake said, gesturing at them and the seat he'd had added to the table, then at Zane. "This is the young man I was telling you about. Today he went far beyond the call of duty, and he wasn't even on duty. Just a citizen volunteer, you might say, willing to risk his life for someone in mortal danger."

"Good job," Stark said, "this country needs more young men like you."

"You sound like an Army recruiter," Zane said.

Muir rolled her eyes—down and dirty even before "hello."

Stark hesitated, not sure if this was meant in jest or as a reproof. In present company, he thought it behooved him to politely chuckle.

Pat Stark said, "I knew about you before your heroics, Zane. Those lovely cactus flowers you gave Muir, I think it was the last time you dined here, honey. She passed them on to me, Zane, and in that earthware vase"—glancing at Blake —"they were so very lovely. And fragile. I so wished they could have lasted longer."

"Yeah," Zane said, "they were kind of a onetime thing."

The waiter came over and laid down a table set in front of the newcomer, adding a menu and wine list.

Blake said, "We've already made our choice. Richardson and I are having chuckwagon steaks and the ladies, brook trout from over in Utah."

"This is our treat," Stark said. "For a job done better than well."

Zane looked at Muir. "He talking about graffiti?"

"Please," she pleaded softly, trying not to have them hear, and then in an almost whisper, "Mind whatever manners you have."

Blake interjected, "These two have a kind of conflictual relationship. Kind of like mine and Pat's was. But here we are, breaking bread together. All wars come to an end sometime."

He looked at Zane, who got the message. Blake was, after all, his boss.

The waiter came back with an iPad to add Zane's order. The latter looked up at him:

"You don't have grilled gorp?"

This baffled the waiter. The others didn't quite know what to say, except for Muir:

"Pretend you're civilized for once, and if you can't do that, remember you're not paying."

Zane nodded, said to the waiter: "The steak and trout, both medium cooked. Kind of a surf and turf thing, you know."

"Those steaks are pretty darn copious, Zane," Stark said.

"We've ordered a white and a red, so we can sample both," Blake said. "But maybe now you've joined the party, we can go one more."

Muir said, "Mr. Bailey lives on branch water, Dad."

"Champagne," Zane said to the waiter. "Bottle, not a glass."

This also gave pause to the others. Zane pointed at the wine list for the waiter.

"Not the Dom. It's good stuff but I prefer the Bollinger."

The waiter nodded and headed off.

"Well," Pat Stark said, "now we'll be able to make a real toast."

"See what you got yourself in for?" Muir said to her father. "Don't say I didn't warn you."

"Bollinger?" He chuckled, "I think I can handle that."

"And cactus flowers too," Pat added.

Zane smiled, enjoying seeing what he gathered was Muir's discomfiture.

"Well, if it's no good," she riposted, "I'm ordering the Dom." To Zane: "Whether you like it or not."

They all laughed, and even Zane smiled.

The waiter brought an ice bucket and the Bollinger champagne, opened.

"Would you care to test it, sir?" he asked Zane.

"I would prefer the ladies do so," he said. "Elegance knows elegance."

"That is so sweet," Pat said, "don't you think so, honey?"

"My mother wants me hitched in the worst way."

Zane smiled at Pat. "And with me she definitely would be, I'm afraid."

"The champagne is delicious," Muir said, sipping.

Zane took his glass and raised it in a symbolic toast.

"To the Grand Canyon."

"Hear hear," Blake said.

They all drank, toasting.

Muir said softly, "May it last forever."

Zane raised his glass and toasted again to her, appreciating her sentiment. "As well, those who love it."

"He really is sweet," Pat said.


After the dinner the group walked out together, Zane Bailey among them, and stood outside the El Tovar entrance to say goodbyes. As none of the others seemed to know quite how to say good night, the once and future Ranger jumped in:

"It's been a pleasure and a learning experience. Thanks."

Pat said, "My gosh, the way Muir talked, I pictured you worse than those French revolutionaries. The ones who chopped off heads, I mean."

"Before they chop, revolutionaries size up their enemies. The size of their throats, I mean."

"Yes," Stark said, "I think I got off easy this night. Probably won't the next time."

"You can go to your bank on that, Richardson," Muir said. "And by the way, check your wallet pocket before you leave."

Blake objected, smiling, "No Ranger of mine steals anything but respect from his opponents. Which he or she has to earn every day. And night. Remains to be seen if you did tonight."

They all said good night and the power couple, finance-wise, went off to the parking lot where Stark's Mercedes waited.

Blake said to Zane and Muir, "You two don't do anything I wouldn't do."

Muir said, "I guarantee you he will. Not me."

Zane asked Blake, "She always been a good little girl like this?"

Blake smiled and turned away. "Looks like truce's over. Good night."

When he'd moved away, Muir said, "I can't believe you made it through a full-course meal without insulting everyone. Especially Richardson Stark. I mean, I've been tougher on him than you."

"Saving my ammo."

At first he hadn't, launching in when Richardson Stark began extolling the Canyon and how it could be developed.

"Blake'll tell you he's in dire need of funding, and he is. But the answer isn't more government, with all due respect. It's private enterprise. There's no reason our parks can't make money."

Blake Wilson countered, "If Richardson had his way, he'd build an elevator from rim to river."

"Yes, with glass walls, so everybody--the elderly, the handicapped, the poor who can't afford a pair of hiking shoes--can see this great spectacle. I'm talking all Americans."

"And the cost of the ride? The hamburger stands you'll want to build at both ends?"

"Take one of those helicopter rides you love so much," Zane jumped in. "When you see those sandstone walls and wildflowers and little cascades, try to imagine it all littered with Styrofoam cups, plastic straws and cheap mustard. I was just a little kid, hadn't even learned to talk yet, when Blake Wilson chained himself to that boulder in the middle of the Colorado. Two weeks in the middle of winter, pretty near died of exposure. I remember thinking, Is this what it means to be a man? One hell of a man?"

Pat looked pained. "I didn't sleep for two weeks. He had a wife and two-year-old daughter depending on him and here he was ready to sacrifice them for a bunch of concrete."

She exchanged a long look with Blake in the awkward silence. Finally he said, quietly:

"It turned out all right in the end, didn't it? Everybody got what they wanted."

Now Zane said to Muir, "After that the ammo went right back into the can. He didn't need me to reopen old wounds, not when he had so many forces around the table arrayed against him."

"That's where you're wrong, as usual. I love my father and I'll protect him against anything and anybody who tries to hurt him. Even myself. Good night. And even if some people think you're so sweet, remember what I said about armed security."

She headed off, just able to still hear him say, despite their continuing philosophical differences:

"Let's do this again sometime. Around a campfire."

She turned back to say: "I bought a new stove. Don't need you any more."

And continued walking.

## Harvey's Campfire Program

Harvey Pine was ecstatic to see how many campers and tourist passersby had gathered for his campfire program tonight, whose main theme centered on the Grand Canyon squirrel.

"I'm sure you folks have encountered these little critters already. I call them critters, kids, which is short for 'creatures,' because they were created like us to enjoy the natural world, and when I speak about the natural world, as a Ranger here I'm talking about—"

He waited, hoping for a response, and though a number of persons look puzzled or too shy to venture a response, a youngster named Lee finally piped up, "The Grand Canyon!"

"Bravo kiddo. Let's congratulate er…"

"Lee."

"A big hand for Lee!"

Applause duly came, especially from Lee's friends, a group of it seemed all races and denominations.

A girl in the group added, "One of them stole my granola bar!"

"Well now we shouldn't say stole because you see, the Canyon squirrel continually has to forage for his food. Otherwise he can't survive. But we really don't want you to give food to them, and you know why?"

This didn't get an answer, as Harvey imagined, so he quickly explained:

"They get used to handouts, and sometimes they eat plastic and other noxious elements that destroy their digestive system. So if one of them took a handful of gorp, it means he ate a food product that was excellent for his health. Sounds to me like he was a pretty smart customer."

"I've heard they're dangerous," said a man who seemed to Harvey to hail from India. Why else would he be wearing a turban here in the Great Outdoors? he reasoned to himself.

"Only if you get too careless with a handout. Then they don't distinguish too well the difference between gorp and a man's—or woman's—fingers. Yet another reason, folks, to let them live and let them let us live. Got that?"

He chuckled, both because he found this funny and because he hoped it would animate them. But tonight's crowd looked curious and ready to learn but feeling the effects of a long day hiking or sightseeing. Lee and the group of kids looked mildly interested, but only a few tore themselves away very long from their cellphones and the wide Web world. Harvey knew he'd have to be on his game tonight, even more than most, so he launched into a surefire crowd-pleaser.

"Now that brings us to the Kaibab squirrel. Did you know, the Kaibab squirrel lives on the North Rim of the canyon? The only place on earth where you can find those cute little critters with the white tail. It's their beloved home over there, among the Ponderosa pines where they can feast on pine nuts all year long. Let me tell you, Snickers bars aren't their thing, so gobble up that chocolate in peace. Leave them alone and they'll leave you alone."

"Let them live and let them let us live," Lee chimed in.

Harvey was momentarily knocked off his program by this, but recovered quickly. "Rangers got to be prepared for action and even more importantly, all kinds of feedback," he liked to say.

"Right you are, Lee. Another big hand for Lee, folks!"

The boy beamed with pleasure as the crowd applauded him. It was getting late and Harvey saw this as a good moment to wrap up and wish them all a "very happy tomorrow."

From the looks of them, they were tired but from having enjoyed the day, and he trusted he'd added to their happiness.

The only "fly in my ointment, even though I don't use ointment and it's just an expression," he said to himself, is I was expecting to be filmed by a Mr. Joe Blevins for his You-Tube channel. He'd solicited me hard, even though I didn't need persuasion, planning to put my campfire program as episode end and teaser for the next.

But Harvey scanned the crowd several times and saw not a trace of Mr. Blevins. He found that painful and disrespectful, though later, when he'd reflected, he realized Joe Blevins could have had an accident. Slipped off a trail or something.

Time and tomorrow would tell.

"Everybody sleep well under the light of those Western stars!" Harvey concluded.

# The Senator Arrives

A new dawn at the Canyon. Each day brought new challenges and new opportunities, and Blake Wilson saw both today in the person of Senator Perceval J. Graham, Chairman of the Congressional Committee that oversaw funding for the national parks and Interior Department.

He announced to his early morning gathering of available troops: "The Senator's taking the train up from Williams. Once he gets here, he's away from Washington politics, special interest lobbies, pro-development types and some assistants who might not know the Grand Canyon from Grand Central Station. We've got his attention for one solid day. Let's make our case."

Harvey lamented, "You haven't got him down for my campfire program. I'm discussing the different varieties of cactus. Congressmen don't hear that every day."

Blake smiled. "We'll see."

Josh noted, "You've assigned me and Lucinda to hold his hand. But I'm East Coast, just like him."

"Right, you're his homesick remedy."

Zane Bailey was back in uniform, and he contributed what passed for him as an exceedingly mellow comment: "I'll take him in hand. He needs a history lesson."

It occurred to him that his young colleagues might need same.

"You remember that dam they almost built right in the middle of the canyon? Worst boondoggle in the history of greedy assaults on the wilderness. He was just a young Congressman then. He voted for it."

Blake countered, "And now he's chairman of the committee that oversees funding for our national parks. I'm more concerned about how he's going to vote next."

Lucinda concurred, pointedly to Zane, "You attack him, he's liable to take a helicopter down to Flagstaff for the Off Road Vehicle race."

"I've got something to say about ORV's, too."

Blake tried to calm the waters. "Sure, I know you'd love to fill his ear. So would I. We're understaffed, underpaid and unappreciated, and his committee wants to make cutbacks. We need his support. Now's not the time to rattle his cage."

"That why you've sent me to Timbuktu?" Zane asked.

"That trail on the Tonto is crumbling bad. Somebody's got to repair it."

"Conciliation, not confrontation. That's your philosophy, isn't it?"

"For now. And since I'm head man, that's the policy we'll follow."

End of discussion.

The troops dispersed to go about their duties.

Zane headed for the General Store. He arrived just a few minutes after opening, and as he began stuffing his backpack with provisions for the day and after, some canned--peaches, beef stew--but mostly lightweight freeze-dried and a few strips of beef jerky, all certified organic, preferably by more than one legit organization, he noticed another customer dressed in trendy fashion hiking boots without a smudge on them, Jodhpur pants, and hat more suitable for a luxury safari than a mule train.

Muir was loading a stylish daypack with plastic-wrapped sandwiches and Coca-Cola Lites and just generally, all the foods he detested.

As usual Muir was not thrilled to see him, and less so when he moved over to her as she was cashing out her groceries.

Last night's truce seemed so…last night.

Zane said, provocatively as per, "All that junk food, hell of a sugar rush. Who's your client today, the Easter Bunny?"

"I'm not surprised you still believe in him. Most infantile men do."

"If you're so grown up, why are you rotting your teeth and system with those chemicals? That's what it all is, you know. Additives and artificial sugars. Guaranteed to cause obesity. Get near a match and you're liable to explode."

"There are worse things to get next to."

He whistled. "Got those fangs out today. Stray bone from the trout last night stick in your craw? Or just some of the company at table?"

"Not that I care one second for your opinion, but I'm taking some school children into the canyon on the mule train. These are their snacks."

"Their parents can't afford dried fruit?"

"Frankly, no. They're inner city kids. We're sponsoring their vacation here. We do things like that sometimes, when we're not raping the land and exploiting innocent taxpayers."

A man came in, wearing shorts, boots, a souvenir shop T-shirt and hat that would normally be worn by an oldster whose only idea of a fashion runway led to a country club golf course.

He had clothes on now, but Zane recognized the soapless man.

Danny G. said—to Muir, not Zane for whom he cared less than less:

"Excuse me. You happen to know when the mule train's leaving? The drover must be taking a pee somewhere. I'm anxious to see that darn Canyon."

Muir said, "He's waiting for me. You're right. It's past time we get going."

She started to move away. Danny G. fell in step.

"You're coming with? Hot diggety dog. Carry your pack for you? You're real loaded down there, maybe need more than two hands."

She gave it to him to lug, a broad smile on her face. She looked back at Zane.

"Well, a real gentleman. We could use more like you around here."

Danny G. winked back at Zane who didn't appreciate it. "Looks like this mule train's leaving you behind, Hoss."

Zane glowered and had a parting word as they walked away.

"Careful the mule doesn't mistake you for a chamber pot."

This time Danny G. whistled, but this was for Muir. "That what they call courtesy from US National Park employees?"

"He's on probation. And it's not going to stick."

"Wouldn't know about probation. I'm Mr. Solid Citizen, if I do say so for myself. Soon as I pay my last parking ticket, I mean. Hey, how long before we get to the bottom?"

"A few hours."

"What's the matter, they got lead in their saddlebags?"

"You don't want to rush the mules. You know, one missed step…"

"Yeah, safety first. It's the hikers, they're the problem. They clog the trail, take their own sweet time. That wrangler's got a whip, he ought to use it. A little pop against their ear…whop!"

"Are you serious?"

"I was raised on a ranch. A human's just like any other animal. Need goosin' from time to time. If not always."

Zane watched them go, surprised at the level of distaste he felt for her so-called gentleman. And surprised he'd found enough restraint. After all, it wouldn't do to punch out someone his first day back on the job.

Unless they really deserved it, he told himself.

When Muir and her new companion reached the Bright Angel trailhead, the inner-city kids were gathered there waiting for the wrangler to finish checking out the mule train about to head down. The youths, a real polyglot of races, were all mounted or mounting on the placid, sure-footed mules. As they came up, the spunky Lee perked up even more than his usual.

"Hey, our guide."

All the youngsters' eyes turned toward Danny G, who looked uneasy with this attention and hastily pointed to Muir.

"Her. I'm along for the ride, like you buckaroos."

Lee responded, "What's a buckaroo?"

Muir jumped in, "Cowboys and cowgirls, just like you're going to be after this ride. I'm Muir and I'm sure happy to meet you all. Ready for some fun?"

Excited cries in the affirmative.

"Well let's get this trail drive going."

She turned toward the wrangler. "How's it going, John?"

"Saddle up and we'll see how it goes. Glad to have you along, Muir. Been a long while."

"Yeah, but you can't take the canyon out of the girl."

"And who'd want to?"

Lee piped up again: "Hey, a Ranger!"

Zane had come up. He smiled wide as he could and said, "Hey, kids, welcome to the most beautiful canyon on earth, maybe the universe. Sure wish I could come with you today."

Some groaned.

Muir had frowned, an expression that said, Did this guy have to follow her everywhere? But she welcomed his travel plans or lack therof.

"You on litter duty today, Mr. Ranger?"

"We call it trail reconstruction."

"Moving rocks and brush. Too bad. Well, somebody has to do it. And on a day when a United States Senator comes visiting."

Zane let the sarcasm slide and advised the group, "Sit back easy in the saddle, kids. No jumping around or getting off your mount without previewing the wrangler. These mules are trained to stay on the trail. In fifty years we've never lost a rider."

Danny G said to Lee: "Better tighten this cinch, pardner. Here's how you do it."

Muir said pointedly to Zane, who was disappointed to see that Danny G did in fact know what he was doing: "Looks like we're in good hands. But thank the Ranger for his advice anyway, kids."

They did so in a scattering of voices.

John the drover said to Danny G, checking his list, "You'd be Mr. Blevins?"

"Call me Joe." He mounted his mule.

Muir added, this also for her nemesis: "Halfway down we'll stop for a soda and cookies, kids."

A much more animated series of eager cries greeted this. Zane steamed as the mule train headed away and down. Muir smiled back, seeing how well she'd goaded him. Danny G started singing a cowboy song.

Zane watched the mule train till it disappeared around a bend of the Bright Angel, then shouldered his backpack and headed down behind them toward the Tonto Trail. He'd be inhaling some trail dust, but he realized with some surprise that it would definitely stick in his craw less than the sight of Muir riding beside Mr. Blevins.

At the terminus of the Grand Canyon railroad, Blake Wilson, Lucinda and Josh waited with some press people, curious spectators and a horde of tourists gathered for the return trip to Williams and points beyond as the train arrived.

Behind a very attractive female assistant and an eager young male aide, the Senator stepped down, a rotund man who clearly had been living very well off the fat of the land.

Blake moved forward to greet him, extending his hand for a shake.

"Welcome to the Grand Canyon, Senator. I'm Blake Wilson, Head Ranger."

The Senator chuckled. "You don't have to tell me who you are. I remember you from that dam fight. You still the same hellraiser you were then?"

Josh and Lucinda exchanged looks.

"That was a long time ago," Blake responded, also chuckling.

"Lot of water under the bridge, eh? At least that thing got built, didn't it?"

"Yes sir. Thin steel girders, wood planking...blends in perfectly with the landscape and lets people cross the river safely. A sound environmental decision."

He led the Senator out of the crowd toward their waiting vehicles.

Blake drove with the Senator in the front seat with him. In back were Josh, Lucinda and the Senator's two assistants.

The Senator said, "Susie's never seen the Canyon, would you believe that?

"And I'm from Phoenix!" Susie laughed.

Not one for political correctness, the Senator said, "The Lord did a good job endowing her, but He forgot curiosity."

She growled, "And you forgot your smarts today. If you ever had them. That is so sexist."

Battered by this reproof, the Senator managed to feebly respond, "I'm trying to learn. Hell, that's why I'm here today."

The Congressman left the field of battle and turned for refuge to business. "Blake, you've got to understand my position. Every day I've got government and civil service lobbyists asking for more funding. Nobody ever seems to have enough."

"Senator, what I'd like to have you understand and report back to your colleagues on the Committee is, my Rangers don't just hand out brochures and give campfire talks, important as those activities are. The Grand Canyon is a town. You've got permanent residents, you've got thousands of visitors pouring in every day from every corner of the world. Somebody's got to police it, run it, save it when natural disaster strikes. But it's also a wilderness. Thousands of square miles of up and down terrain, some of it where no man has ever set foot. I guarantee you, it takes more than a mop and broom."

On the Bright Angel Trail he mule train wound down a long curve. Danny G groused, "No wonder these jackasses never lost a man. I've rode dead horses that go faster."

Lee couldn't stop wondering about this man in cowboy hat and boots riding next to him.

"Are you a real cowboy, mister?"

Danny G answered, "I used to be. Gave it up."

He looked at Muir, wanting her to hear this. "Out there on the range with nothing but coyotes and steers for company, a man gets tired of the lone prairie. Starts missing the ladies."

Something about the way he said this unsettled her. She had to force a grin.

She said, "You're sure anxious to get down. Liable to miss the scenery. You have a hot date or something?"

Danny G gave her a shiteating grin: "Not yet."

Muir turned away from him. Down below, still some 1000 meters of descent, she saw for the first time the architect of the wondrous rock sculptures they were riding through, the Colorado River.


At the intersection where the east-west Tonto Trail crossed the Bright Angel, Zane paused to watch the mule train pass out of his line of sight. He knew that if he kept watching, at a certain point it would come into view again. But he had work to do.

Frankly he doubted that the Tonto needed much if any repair work, but he knew damn well that Blake Wilson wanted him far and wide and mostly, many moons and miles away from a Senator who would not appreciate a relentless eco-activist bending his ear.

Maybe literally.

He understood, and that tomorrow was another day and the Senator planned to stay overnight. Who knew what the evening and tomorrow would bring in the way of buttonholing opportunities.

In the meantime, he had the glories of the Tonto to occupy him—and glories they were in terms of solitude and eye-filling panoramas—and hopefully, take his mind away from that mule train.

The Senator had mounted a podium wrapped in bunting, as was the entire overlook where iron rails served as barriers for the too-eager. He now had a crowd to address in front of him, and no worry about the wide, deep canyon behind him where his words might be lost in the wind and sun and flapping of condor wings.

"I've heard some people say--some politicians--if you've seen the Grand Canyon once, you've seen it all. Yes, incredible as it seems. Well, I haven't been to all the fine overlooks here on the South Rim of this magnificent Canyon, but this new one, built with your taxpayer dollars and maintained by the elite force of Park Rangers—well I think you'll all join me in saying, 'Great job, gentlemen and ladies!' "

Hearty applause seconded his tribute. Nearby Blake stood with Lucinda and Josh. The Rangers acknowledged the applause with smiles and waves.

"For this overlook," the Senator continued, "one word and one word only comes to mind: 'Awesome.' I am reminded of the words of the great Theodore Roosevelt, father of our national park system. About the Grand Canyon he said, 'You cannot build on it. You cannot improve it. Leave it alone.' To which I say, 'Bully!'"

More fervent applause.

Afterward Blake came up to the Senator and said,

"Appreciate your help and warm words, sir."

The Senator nodded and smiled. "Nothing that wasn't one thousand per cent deserved." He shook the Head Ranger's hand vigorously, perhaps too much so.

When Blake turned away, the Senator looked toward the photographer nearby snapping away, asked softly of his assistants: "He get that?"

Next stop on the Senator's itinerary: the park museum at the Center. Lucinda and Josh were showing the Senator around the exhibits of geological strata, early man at the Grand Canyon, Anasazi artifacts, and mock-ups of animal life.

Harvey Pine had joined them and was eagerly tagging behind, hoping for a chance to get in a word to the Senator.

Lucinda explained, "We call them Anasazi, the 'Ancient Ones.' A thousand years ago they had a flourishing society throughout the Southwest. They built cliff dwellings like Mesa Verde and granaries like this one. One day they just disappeared. Nobody knows why or where they went. Maybe they were ancestors of the Navajo and Hopi people. Maybe not."

"It's a mystery we'd like to solve," Josh added. "For all sorts of reasons but mainly, climate change."

Lucinda said, "If they made a mistake and exhausted all their natural resources, we don't want to repeat it."

Josh: "A lot of these archaeological sites have been destroyed or looted by vandals. We'd like to preserve them all but--not enough manpower."

Lucinda got to the bottom line, "Just one or two more Rangers would make a lot of difference."

The Senator had been listening carefully, and it seemed to them that they'd bent his ear favorably. He began "Well now, maybe I can—"

"Mr. Senator—"

Harvey thrust forward his hand. "Harvey Pine. Chief park naturalist and interpreter. I'm giving a campfire talk tomorrow night on cactus. I'd be honored if you could join our jolly bunch."

"Well er—" the Senator said, looking to his assistants for rescue.

"Sir, you've got to prep for the event in Flagstaff," the assistant Susie rescued.

Relieved, the Senator said, "Yeah, some sort of road vehicle thing, can't miss it. Constituents, you know. Tell you what, why don't you send me a brochure. I'll read it first thing."

Harvey beamed: "Yes sir, you got it!"

Recognizing a nerd when he saw one, the Senator took his assistant's arm and ushered her away, ostensibly to view other Visitor Center exhibits.

Lucinda and Josh, if looks could kill, would have had Harvey laid out already.

As it was, Lucinda had to make do with a shot off her colleague's bow: "You won't make the campfire either, because I'm going to break your neck." She moved away, furious.

Josh followed; "No, let's cut out his tongue and feed it to a Kaibab squirrel."

Harvey said, baffled, "What'd I do?"


In the hospital Heinz woke up from one of his frequent naps this day and the last to see Nadja watching over him, as she'd been doing since his admittance. He smiled at her and she looked wonderfully joyed to see him able to do it.

"Bring me some paper and a pen."

"Heinz, I don't think—"

"Yes. We must catch this fucking bastard."

Ordinarily Nadja would have protested, but she'd never heard him talk like that. She went looking.

The mule train wound down toward the Colorado, and the erstwhile cowboy had managed to dismount and mount again, no doubt by coincidence climbing back into the saddle as Muir passed by. He fell into line behind her.

He sallied, "Your name as cute as you are?

"It's Muir. My father named me after the great conservationist. But being a cowboy, you'd know that."

"My old man named me after an ex-con who liked to rob churches. Had a real sense of humor, my old man Yours must've liked the Great Outdoors. He a Ranger like Mr. Greenjeans back there?"

"Sort of. He's the head Ranger. He runs the park!"

Danny G took this in with more than a little interest.

"No lie…"

Down below they saw a rafting party coming in to a landing across the river just as they themselves approached the end of the trail at the Colorado. A bridge spanned the river, and the drover led them toward it.


In the Ranger office, Missy noticed an unusual text message. She double checked the number.

"Our shellshocked tourist Heinz is getting better. He's profiling our suspect."

Blake came over, took a look at the sketch she downloaded. It was rough.

"Can we work with this?" she asked her boss.

"It's a start," Blake Wilson answered. "Send it out."

## A Rat on the River

At the Colorado River, riders and rafters were mingling. The mule train had reached the river, crossing over the bridge that allowed access and made for wonderful photo ops. Muir had taken deep satisfaction in the kids' cries of delight when they'd realized they'd made it down and now had the mighty river that nourished more than one Western state under their bootstraps.

This was what the trip was all about. If one couldn't bring Nature to the inner city, well...

Near Phantom Ranch a few short minutes later she announced to the kids, "Lunch at the Phantom Ranch. Last one there doesn't get ice cream."

They all took off running, shouting and yelling. Muir turned to some of the rafting party, a sunburned group whose city paunches had not been worn off by their past few days on the river.

"Sorry, folks. Didn't want you to get trampled in the stampede."

One of the rafters with a strong Bronx accent said, "Watch yourself, lady. Here we go."

They needed no sweets motivation of any kind and hurried as best they could toward the ranch too.

Muir headed down to the river where Dock Curry was tying up the rafts.

Danny G kept his eye on her...and the rafts.

Muir asked, "Hey, Dock. How's the rapids?"

"Like I like 'em: mean."

"Must be letting more water out from the dam."

"That or it's leaking. Beer's that way, folks."

The last members of the rafting group started heading toward the ranch.

Dock said, "Couple hours of civilization, they'll be screaming to get back to the river. But we're camping here tonight."

"I better join my herd. Join us for lunch, Dock?"

"Soon as I tie up."

She moved away and Dock proceeded to do just that. He noted Danny G hovering nearby, eavesdropping and watching.

"She is one pretty lady," Danny said to Dock. "I think we got a thing going. Got kind of close on the way down, life stories and all that. Wouldn't mind taking a raft trip with her. Love Boat, you know what I mean?"

"Muir's always ready to smooth the ride for visitors. She was great working for me. Wish I could have kept her."

"A river guide too. Man, does she have some skills."

"Yeah, but falling in love at first sight isn't in her playbook, know what I mean?"

Danny G smiled. "First time for everything. Dock. Hey, how fast these suckers go? If it's not like a state secret."

"Current's around 4 miles an hour. You want to go faster, got to put in the elbow grease."

"And run those rapids. Some job, eh?"

"I like it."

"Me, you couldn't pay me enough. Nursemaiding a bunch of tenderfeet who wouldn't know a paddle from a chopstick. Every last one of 'em thinks they're on a big adventure. A lot of fat guts sitting on a raft, rubber squeaking like they let out a fart. Like they don't fart plenty like it is."

"Sounds like you swallowed some mule dust. Grab a beer, it'll chill you out."

Danny G knew he'd been insulted, but after a moment, realized it wasn't the time or place to react. He forced a smile.

"Yeah. Bright idea."

It was lunchtime. Muir was in the middle of happy kids, all eating ice cream and drinking sodas after their meal. She was having a good time, too.

Lee and another boy were giving Twinkies to a Grand Canyon squirrel, which showed no fear.

Muir asked him, "You ever played in a waterfall?"

"I've never even seen one. I didn't bring my swimsuit."

"Shorts will do just fine."

"Outstanding!"

Lee yelped as the squirrel suddenly snatched a morsel of twinkie .

Muir said, "They're spoiled."

Lee responded, "I didn't know. I've never had the problem. Being spoiled I mean."

Muir reflected a moment on the young boy's wisdom before smiling warmly at him.

"You will on this trip," she said. "I guarantee it."

Nearby, Dock came up from the river and joined his party of rafters, who were enjoying the fruits of civilization in the form of ice-cold beer.

One of them hurried over, asked a question to which Dock replied:

"Naw, cell phones don't work too good down here. Used to have a public phone but it got uprooted you might say. Now if you can catch a satellite on its way over..."

The rafter said, in a worried tone, "We're like cut off from the world!"

Dock ironized, "Yeah. Big loss."

Muir was watching Danny G. She'd seen him with your basic burger and fries which he'd wolfed down. Despite his attempt at camaraderie with Lee, he'd made no effort to interact with the youngsters.

Dock had been watching, too. He came up to her and said, "You meet all kinds, and some you wished you'd said goodbye to before hello."

Muir nodded. "He's got a John Wayne fixation." Then added, "And John Wayne he ain't."

She turned her attention to her charges.

"Ready to hit the trail again, kids?"

They all shouted a vociferous assent. A short time later they'd mounted their mules under John's direction, along with the half-dozen lucky tourists who'd managed to reserve this special trip far in advance.

One mule remained riderless.

"Changed your mind, Mr. Blevins?" John asked.

Danny G looked surprised. "About what?"

"You asked permission to film Ribbon Falls, said it would make a highlight for your social media followers. But if you're bushed, no problem. Ranch has got lots of beer."

"Naw, I got energy to burn, except my backside you know, it took a whupping and I got to rest it up for the trip back. I'll be fine, just gonna hang around watching Ol' Man River."

Danny G had no clue where they were going, but he said to himself, right there I did some deft pirouette—even the sexy schoolmarm didn't look sideways at him. Or so he thought. She wasn't all cheesecake.

She climbed into the saddle.

"Don't do anything I wouldn't do," he said to her, without smiling.

"I kind of think that isn't a lot," she responded.

As the mule train headed off, he confirmed to himself, yep, got to watch that cowgirl real close like.

Muir on the other hand completely forgot about Mr. Blevins as she rode up the North Kaibab Trail with her lively charges. He was your typical obnoxious type whose come-ons went past her like a bad odor—out of smell, out of mind. She'd met hundreds like him in her past, men who made Zane Bailey look like the Prince of Wales and beyond.

Besides, she had all she could do to manage the excitement and endless questions of the kids. They'd been all agog and maybe a bit intimidated by the Canyon coming down, but now they knew her and their mule carriers and felt relaxed. And, she thought, delighted by where they were and what they were doing.

So she answered their questions and anticipated more by pointing out the cactus and other vibrant plants that grew everywhere.

"That's ocotillo," she said to Lee, and loud enough for the others to hear. "I love that name. Look at how it blooms in the sand. It doesn't care about the heat and wind and dust, it just keeps on living and growing. Who says you can't grow good and strong in the desert? Like, don't talk to me about where I came from, look where I'm going, up toward that beautiful sun."

Lee said, "Is that like, poetry?"

"Yeah," one of his companions chimed in, "like you, a poet who don't know it."

"I know it," Lee countered.

Another boy joined in and they ganged up on Lee, just this side of too much, and Muir monitored the raillery closely to see that it didn't descend into worse.

Just as Lee came back at them with, "You people need help," Muir was able to raise her voice:

"Cascade!"

They had turned off the main Kaibab Trail and ascended, and then there it was suddenly, a Ribbon Falls indeed, the water plunging down in a long thin stream to the rock desert below.

They spent 2 hours gamboling over, under and around the "blessing, the miracle of water," as Muir put it to the kids when their energy finally started to wear down and they were capable of listening and concentrating for five minutes. She'd asked if they'd had fun and after the fun screaming faded, she gave them a lesson in ecology and how important it was to appreciate and preserve and protect the one element on earth and in nature without which none of them would be there.

"Water," she said. "A magic word. On the way back I want you all to repeat it more than once, out loud. Ok? Deal?"

"WATER" they all yelled in agreement.

When Muir had gotten her charges organized and camped and ready for the "evening chowdown, followed by songs and stories," she ambled down to see Dock. His charges had put up for the night at the Ranch, a mid-raft trip luxury he liked to reserve for them, and he was heading off to join them. "Anything to get away from this Blevins character. What hole did he crawl out of? I mean, if he asked me once he asked me a hundred times what it was like to run a rapid."

"Fast. That's all you needed to say."

"Not with him. I've got a feeling he hankers to take the oars himself, like one of those guys who spends a million to go up in space."

"Except they're not piloting. He's the kind, a mile downstream he'll start spouting BS and forget which end of the paddle to use."

"Copy that, I'm with you there. Want to join us for a couple of beers?"

"My boys and girls wouldn't let me, and to tell you the truth Dock, tonight I can skip your tall tales about running Lava Falls with one oar tied behind you."

"And there you're wrong. Last time we flipped over and that's one hairy story."

"You flipped? I mean, Lava's a bear but I don't believe it. Hey, I'll make it up to you by keeping Mr. Blevins in camp."

"For which I'll owe you big time."

Muir found it easy to monitor Mr. Blevins. She already knew he was an enigma, and he reinforced that analysis by hanging out with her and the kids throughout the evening, seeming to enjoy the tales and songs and repartee and camaraderie—even joining in from time to time with comments that were less off the wall than hereto and, she thought, more in his character. Later she surmised that he joined the fun for a more basic reason: to cadge a few hot dogs and cokes and the other goodies purchased for the group. Occupied with the kids and wanting to maintain a goodfellow ambiance, she hadn't objected—and he did his part for the ambiance.

Later too she remembered he hadn't specified where he was spending the night—at Phantom Ranch or camped along with them at the campsite—though she hadn't noticed any of his gear.

At any rate, at the time, she didn't react immediately when he left the fun and headed off into the night.

At the river one could almost hear the swift current that was plain and visible on this moonlit night, despite the campsite gathering and, more distant, the fainter laughter and chatter from the Ranch where Dock and his rafters were finishing dinner.

Danny G was untying a raft. When the moor rope came loose, he started to ease it away from its partner rafts to which it was also lashed. Just as Danny G got in--

"Tired of mule travel?"

Danny G didn't turn. Just listened. He knew who it was.

Muir continued

"The only thing dumber than stealing is heading down this river alone. At night. If you don't know what you're doing, first rapid and you're sausage."

Danny G whirled. He leveled his gun at her.

"Yeah. I'm hiring me a guide who damn well better know her shit."


It didn't take long for them to glide down the river, and Muir had little reason to row. She handled the oars deftly, keeping them straight and true as was possible. But...

"Once that moon moves over the cliffs in about 15 minutes, we're going to be traveling in darkness, like the primeval kind. I won't be able to read the rapids and we'll flip. A few minutes in that water and hypothermia will set in. If you don't know what that means, I'll tell you flat out. You won't even be able to use your lips to cry for help. Not that that would do you any good. Understand? Dead man floating."

Muir had enough light still to see him smirking.

He came back with, "I won't ask if you think I'm stupid 'cause I know you do. You just keep rolling along. Old Dock the river rat probably thought I gave a shit about his sermons. 'Respect the river' and that kind of crap."

He smiled, or rather, a kind of shit-eating grin.

"And all the while he's stashing his gear real good and handy, so I could see what a big organized pro boatman he is. Impress this tenderfoot he wouldn't let on his boat if I paid him double, which I wouldn't do even if he had this gun. Like he has this flashlight stashed under that canvas right there so big and bright some phony Hollywood star'd kill for it. Guess what. I am ready to kill for it. If I have to. But I got this feeling you're gonna keep on keeping on even when that moon says goodbye for the night, because I'm gonna light our way."

"Not good enough. His light. I've seen it. You can spot a beaver if you have to but a lighthouse beam it is not."

"Gonna have to do."

It did for some long river miles. Muir rowed into the night and thanked the fates that she could see enough to guide the raft. Danny G had fastened Dock's "big-ass beam light" to the raft's prow and it functioned as a headlight.

She said, "Except cars got two headlights, and they paint lines you've got to follow."

"You're doing fine, with my help of course."

As the last words left his mouth, they heard a low rumble up ahead.

"That what I think it is?" Danny G asked.

"Get ready for a midnight swim."

He thought a long moment.

"Pull over."

"Pull over where?"

"To the bank, right or left I don't give a damn."

She did so, and once they'd left the current and glided to the bank, rocky and unsuitable for tents or even a ground mattress, he said, "Tie us down to that boulder."

In a moment Muir was able to anchor the raft.

"Beddy bye," Danny G said, and lay back on the canvas gear, put up his legs and leaned the back of his head on the rubber prow.

"Make yourself comfortable."

"Like that's possible."

"Like I care. Keep to your side, that's all you got to worry about. You come over here, I might let my happy trigger finger go off. Anyway, I don't feel like screwing tonight."

Muir settled in as best she could.

"Have a bad night," she barked. "As in, your worst nightmares."

"Just pray you ain't in 'em."


Zane Bailey cast a thought Muir's way as he settled in to his Ranger bunk for the first time in weeks, ever since his suspension. It was lean and spartan, but nothing like his nightly bunks in the wild. Tonight he would sleep here, a kind of symbolic rejoining of the Ranger community. But he had no intention of ending his camping evenings. He would alternate.

Besides, camping outdoors where no one would think to find him suited him excellently when he had a little foray to make, as in, splashing graffiti on commercial properties that needed most urgently to be reminded of their obligations toward Mother Earth.

And, he thought to himself, so did Muir. And he was just the man to remind her.

Full of contradictions, he had to admit with some chagrin that he regretted not being able to do so up close and personal, as in, sharing her sleeping bag.

Warm spring nights could do that to a man's principles.

## PART 2

# A Kidnapper ID'd

Missy Martin had arrived at the park offices early, 6 am, to monitor radio traffic and incoming email.

"Mr. Wilson?"

She was stunned to see that her boss had beaten her to the office, and she wondered if he might even have slept there. She didn't have to fire up their computer. It was already fired up.

"No IDs yet," Blake said, "but I'd settle for a profile sketch. If that's what you call it."

"It's close enough for them to understand."

"You sure about that?"

"Well, if I can understand it…"

"You're underselling yourself in a big big way. I'm one day on the job and I can see you know your way around the Web. And that's what I need. If only Internet was a trail you could follow by the cairns. Or mini-cairns. Or one rock."

"I'm sure you can do that, sir. I'd follow you."

"For that you deserve a coffee. Yes?"

"Yes. I'll try to light a fire under them. These geek types don't really sleep, you know. Or if they do, it's with their eyes open. Too many screens will do that to you."

Blake got busy with ground roast. He could do that well, having had lots of bachelor experience since his divorce.

He smiled at Missy and quipped, "You seem to have had a lot of messages yesterday, from anywhere and everywhere. Inquiring about the current weather and dewpoint and humidity and by the way, your contact numbers."

"I gave out a lot of dewpoint readings, if that's what you're wondering. I didn't apply for this internship to do a dating scene."

"Well, if I can say anything about dating scenes at the Grand Canyon, you encounter a pretty good class of people on average. From all around the world. Not as many lost souls with baggage enough to sink a battleship. With exceptions, like this guy whoever he is. Tell me if the coffee's satisfactory."

He put down a mug in front of her and she took a sip. She grimaced.

"Too hot?"

"Too strong. It's like, mountain man coffee, yes? Or like, grizzly bear coffee."

"Sorry. My last gig at Yellowstone gave me a bad habit. Trying to discourage animal theft. They'll drink anything if you leave it out. Soften it up with some water."

"No, I need some toughening up. For all those grizzlies out there who wear pants. Hey, something's coming in."

Blake came over, took a look at the printout on the screen. He quickly read the info. Looked worried.

"Grissom. If this is the guy, he's trouble. Photo?"

"Coming up," Missy replied.

Blake pored over the file, looking more worried with each sentence he read.


Harvey Pine was a confirmed bachelor but he knew enough about the birds and bees and young love to respect people's private lives, i.e., in camp tents.

He checked pouch slips every morning to verify payments for campsites and he toured the grounds for the untoward, but he almost never peeked inside visitors' homes for the night—as in the case of a Mr. Blevins.

Harvey did not know the name of the camper—that came later—but he knew the site had been reserved for three nights and on the second morning, he left Mr. Blevins to his pleasure. Harvey assumed it was that. Despite the natural wonders all around, it was not uncommon for lovers to pass some mornings in their tent.

"Making love," he said to himself. "I like to think that because it's so much more classy than 'having sex' or the f-word."

So when he noticed Mr. Blevins' tent shaking from side to side and the sound of grunts and murmurs from inside, he chalked it up to nothing more or less than making love; and he wasn't about to interrupt.

He moved on and went about his business.

The next morning however, this morning, when he came up to Mr. Blevins' tent and found it shaking as before, with the lovemaking grunts even louder, he thought that even if the two lovers inside resembled too-long-deprived bunnies, they perhaps needed a health lesson.

"You folks might think about airing out this tent. I guarantee it'll last a lot longer."

More grunts from inside, some perhaps a little frantic.

"I can open the flap and give you this nice breeze we've got this morning. Yes? No? Up to you, your call. I'm a public servant, you know, and you're my public."

He heard a response in the form of staccato, one might even say muffled, responses. Harvey likened them to a form of Morse code that had to be read.

"I'm going to take that for a yes. Here goes now. Hope you're decent."

He unzipped slowly the principal flap of the tent.

"That better?" The responses went up a decibel level. Harvey reflected.

Dared he look inside?

The clincher came when he reflected that perhaps the denizens here had done something wrong, like uproot a cactus or train a bird to endaround park rules and regulations.

Not about to have that...

He bent down and looked inside.

There was Joe Blevins, lying on his back, mouth taped, hogtied—and hogtied well. Harvey thought, in spite of the urgency before him, that this revelation was a testimony to the efficacy of the US park system. Checks and balances by dedicated public servants like himself.

He said to Joe Blevins, "Dont panic, sir, help is right here, and like they say at Amazon, more on the way."


Heinz entered the Superintendent's Office with Nadja and Blake Wilson let them know how happy he was to see them.

"Looks like you're ready for the trail, the way you're walking," he said to Heinz.

Heinz smiled. "We have full day. Must make up for this lost time."

"The doctors gave him the green light but I want him to see the yellow light," Nadja corrected.

"Yes sir," Blake agreed, "see as much as you can. This canyon will reward you and be here tomorrow, I promise you."

Heinz enthused, "I have second chance at life, now I will appreciate every minute. Not sitting in a big chair."

Nadja changed the subject: "Have you found this man?"

"Working on it. Waiting for a photo that might tell us something. Would you folks mind hanging around a few minutes? For ID?"

Nadja nodded: "We will do this, sure sure."


The Senator strolled in with his assistants and Pat and Richardson Stark.

"I took my Dramamine, Blake, ready for one hell of a ride," he said.

"Think we can guarantee it, Senator. Russ is the best pilot I know and he takes that little helicopter wherever you want to go."

"Well, this here's a private flight, guess you know that. Courtesy of Mr. Richardson Stark and his lovely wife."

Stark smiled. "Blake's going to tell you to leave well enough alone, but I think you'll see there's land aplenty for people to live in harmony with Nature."

Pat looked around.

"Where's our young firebrand?"

"Working the Rim trail. He's not invited today. It wouldn't do to have a knock-down drag-out in a flight over 2 thousand meters of freefall."

"Sounds like a story here," the Senator quipped.

Blake saw Harvey Pine rushing in with Joe Blevins in tow. "Excuse me," he said to the VIPs.

When he moved away Pat Stark said to the Senator, "Our daughter Muir wanted so much to meet you. She's taken some inner city children on an outing into the canyon."

The Senator chuckled. "Frankly, on the scale of importance that ranks a lot higher than palavering with me."

"Stop the presses," Harvey said excitedly to Blake Wilson, "I mean, that's like a metaphor. Sir, this man met our suspect, or I think it's the suspect, that's my deduction."

Joe Blevins raged, "Son-of-a-bitch hogtied me! In my own tent! Excuse my French. You can trace him, he took my phone."

Missy came over, handed Blake her cellphone with a photo. "Tuba City police think he ditched the stolen car they found and caught a ride to the Canyon. He escaped from a prison farm in Arkansas. You might say he's got a rap sheet."

Blake scanned the information on the phone. Turned to Heinz and Nadja.

"Recognize him?"

"Yes, yes!" they echoed together.

"That's the sonofabitch!" Joe Blevins seconded.

Blake turned to his guests, the Senator and the Starks. "Missy makes better coffee than I do. Like to offer you all a cup or two, courtesy of the National Park Service. We've got a situation that can't wait and I've got to make a couple of calls."

Then to Blevins and the Austrians, "Bear with me a few minutes."

They nodded. The Senator said, "No problem, Blake, gives the Dramamine time to settle. Anyway, I got a feeling Richardson's going to be filling my ear."

Stark smiled, "With a whole lot of flattery, sir."

It didn't take long for Blake Wilson to get the info he needed, about the time it took for a leisurely cup of coffee. He announced to his audience of Rangers, guests and victims:

"His name's Danny G Grissom. Or Danny G as he likes to be known. If you're into failed rappers who can't sing and can't rap, he's the ace of aces. You can't say he had an abortive career because he never had a career. The only thing he was good at was plagiarizing other people's songs and making like they were his. Just added his own brand of mediocre lyrics. One day he must have realized that and did what any dangerous loser would, take out his misery on the general public who scorned him. In other words, a life of crime. Mainly holdups but he's gotten worse. Couple of years ago he went on a pistol whipping spree. Convenience store clerk, trucker who gave him a ride, couple of tourists, and when they finally caught him, a police officer. State psychiatrists said they couldn't find a trace of remorse. If he hadn't been stopped...well, he hasn't turned to killing yet that we know of, but he's a man who knows how to use a gun. And likes to."

Heinz nodded.

"He is bad man. Yes?"

"You might say that."

The Senator interjected, "Sounds to me like you've got a perp on the loose here, Blake. If he hasn't skipped town so to speak."

"Yes sir. What we don't like to publicize about our national parks is they sometimes become a refuge for criminals who think we don't have a police force. But we do, and at times like this, we really need them."

As he was speaking, Lincoln Williams and Sheri entered.

"Sir," Lincoln said to Blake, taking him aside to speak privately.

Joe looked increasingly distraught. He'd borrowed Harvey's cellphone.

"He put me on my YouTube channel! Trussed up like Porky Pig ready for somebody's barbecue. These comments, disgusting!"

Harvey soothed, "I know this has been a traumatic experience for you, sir, but we're here to help. We don't have a PTSD counseling service but we do our best to understand pain and life stress. Although admitting that your experience doesn't fall into our usual parameters and response patterns."

"You know how the Web works. It's spread all over the world now!"

"Well, they do say there's no such thing as bad publicity. Not sure I agree, but the world doesn't wait for my opinion. Unfortunately."

"He's ruined my Grand Canyon Odyssey. That's what I call it, my Odyssey, like Homer and all the other great travel writers. Except I write with my camera, you know?"

Harvey nodded, sympathetic, though he noted that Joe was approaching the time where dealing with him brought diminishing returns and others, more needy, would demand his attention. Not to mention, some prep for tonight's campfire program. And not to mention, he had the Senator at elbow's length and he had one heck of a program tonight. It would only take a little cajoling at the right moment...

Joe Blevins continued, "Plus, I missed by mule train ride. One year I've been waiting. It was going to be a highlight of the film!"

"Mule train?" Sheri interjected, overhearing. "Yesterday?"

"Yeah."

Sheri looked at Blake Wilson and his colleagues.

"I checked. Nobody cancelled yesterday."

Joe Blevins looked astonished and momentarily forgot his ordeal. "He took my place?"

"That's possible."

Heinz wondered, "He committed a crime like this for a mule ride?"

Lincoln said cryptically, "Yes and no."

Blake came up to them. The seriousness of his mien cut short the conversation. With Lincoln and Sheri flanking him, he informed:

"We've spotted Danny G Grissom. He went with your mule train down to Phantom Ranch. Some time last night he stole a pontoon raft and apparently headed down the river. To go where, we don't know."

He looked pointedly at Pat.

"It looks like he's taken a hostage."

Pat understood.

"Oh my God, no…"
Blake Wilson and his Rangers moved into double time.

# Into Action

Raymond Gunther at first didn't know what to say when Blake Wilson informed him of what had happened and what he wanted him, Raymond, to do.

"Take over? Well, that's—"

"You've got the experience and you've got the knowhow. I'm going with the chopper team. He's got my daughter and frankly, I couldn't abide sitting here and twisting my guts out with suspense."

"Well..."

"Look, Raymond, I know you've avoided promotions all these years because you love your comfort zone and nobody does what you do better. You're the best advertisement this Canyon's ever had. But I'm counting on you now. Lincoln and Sheri and the others have got to track trail routes and if there's anybody in this crew who can man the office and co-ordinate, it's you."

Raymond again hesitated, but when he finally did find voice he said firmly, "I bounced that little girl on my knee and took her hiking when she got her first pair of boots. Wished I'd had a daughter like her. But it wasn't meant to be. Hell yes you can count on me. These interns I've been training are chomping at the bit. Hell, if they do a better job than me I'll take retirement. And look, don't waste any more time handing me the reins. I'm on it, Chief."

Blake Wilson nodded, convinced.

Lucinda joined Sheri Franklin and Lincoln Williams to huddle with their boss. He remained cool and in charge of himself, but no stress said stress like concern over a child.

"Your thoughts, folks?"

They hesitated.

Blake recognized their reflections and added, "It's my daughter who's been kidnapped, and if there's chances to be taken, I'll take them. Starting with piloting the lead helicopter. What I want from you is objective advice. Your judgements. What's he got in mind, where is he headed, and what are his intentions with his hostage?"

Sheri said, "Well, the obvious conclusion which I know you know Chief is he wants someone else to steer the boat."

Blake countered, "One man can do it. It's oar-powered and it doesn't take a rocket scientist to row. Even running rapids, he could take his chances."

Lincoln said, "I kind of think she got in the wrong place at the wrong time. Had to be down at the river away from the others. Or else, he threatened her. He'll surely have a gun."

Blake reflected a long moment.

"He couldn't be headed for Lake Mead. Too far and too stupid because we can take him there real easy."

"He's got to take out on one of the backcountry trails," Sheri said.

Lincoln added, "Some of which have some unmaintained branches toward the rim. Can we cover them all, that's the question."

"We can damn well try. My job is to spot them from the chopper and narrow down the search. You two organize who goes where. Lucinda, sorry, you'll have to stay at the Backcountry office as per."

"I'd like to monitor a trail, sir."

"Negative. Our law enforcement folks have the training for situations like this. And we need to carry on our regular business if possible."

She didn't look happy, but nodded. As did the others. But Sheri posed a last question.

"Question, sir. Do we want him dead or alive?"

"I think you know that answer."

"And if he comes out solo?"

Blake looked grim, knew the unspoken part of this question.

"If at all possible, alive. If the worst happens, like you say, I'll want to know where my daughter lies."

"Nearest trail they might come out on this Rim is the North Bass. I'll head out there myself."

Janey Ross reacted as Blake Wilson hoped she would to his news. Concerned, angry, goddamn determined to resolve a situation that looked grim but one she was going to handle.

"Not alone," Blake cautioned. "This guy is dangerous and for sure, armed."

"Law enforcement is coming with, but I've got a rifle and know how to use it. I'll move heaven and earth to get him to surrender and only use force as a final option. I'll be thinking about her and her safety at all times, Blake. You can count on me for that."

"I know I can."

"We'll cover the other backcountry trails too. Unless he's a bird he's going to have to use shoe leather and we'll spot him, wherever."

Blake Wilson reflected, moved, finally said with feeling, "I appreciate your dedication, Janey."

He knew already she wasn't the type to swim in cornpone, and she confirmed that by saying, "Sorry I can't stay on the horn, Chief, but North Bass is a ways from here."

"I know you will anyway, but for the record…keep me informed."

When Lily Dawnwind got the call from Blake Wilson, it only took her a half hour to get her gear ready. She never needed to take much food when she hiked, and even though her sentinel duty might go long, she didn't change her habits and stuffed bread and some fried corn and mutton slices. No desserts or sweets—wasn't much into that. Water, yes, even though she'd be hiking along Havasu Creek.

She filled her bottles at the spring pipe near the campground, then set a brisk pace downstream.

She passed Havasu Falls, then skirted the campsites which at this time of day had fewer campers hanging around, as most preferred to hike or swim in the blue-green waters that gave life and spirit to her native canyon.

At Mooney Falls she descended the cliff using the chains and ropes fixed into the rock to aid the climb down and prevent hikers having the same fate as the luckless Mooney, who fell to his death on a short rope, missing the consolation of having such a magnificent cascade named after him. Lily had no inclination or time to wonder if somewhere in the waters some remnants of Mooney had settled, perhaps in a niche or crevice of the calcified rock that formed the stream bed.

Beaver Falls lay about halfway down on her journey, and she reached it in faster time than virtually any pleasure hikers, having grown up in the canyon and done the route many times. Even allowing for spring runoff and the occasional flood that made stream crossings more or less an adventure, she knew them all and where to place her steps.

At Beaver Falls she left the higher cascades behind, but still the crystalline water poured off in ledge after ledge in the creek, almost like a chorus singing her to her destination.

She wanted to reach it sooner rather than later, and she arrived at the Colorado River in what she thought was record time for her.

She scanned the river. No sign of any raft. Early spring did not bring many river runners, but her job today was to spot one in particular. She knew it was too soon for a raft carrying Muir Wilson to arrive, and she did not quite know what she could do except report back to Blake if she saw it.

But she also knew her most important duty: if the raft passed, to check if Muir was alive.

She settled in, seating herself on the grass at a point on the bank above the confluence of Havasu Creek and the Colorado.

Watching and waiting.


Pat Stark had managed to regain some composure, under the ministrations of her husband and the Senator and his assistants, who hovered around her, ever-ready to help. But each time Blake Wilson approached, she recoiled, afraid it would be devastating news.

But this time he simply said, "Let's go."

# Trackdown

On the river Danny G kicked back, sipping a beer, enjoying the float, letting Muir do the rowing.

"Faster, baby doll. I got me a date."

"There's the worst rapids on the river ahead. You ever heard of Lava Falls? Some days that's a Class V. Unrunnable. If you're counting on me to get you through—"

With her foot, she lifted up a life preserver from the bottom of the raft, kicked it over to him.

"—don't. You're gonna need this. I sell houses for a living. Real estate."

Danny G smirked, "Yeah, a real shut-in. And you're trying hard to row like one. But I'm figuring a little girl named 'Muir,' her daddy taught her a thing or two about the Great Outdoors. Straighten us out."

He leveled the gun at her. He looked serious. "Don't kid yourself I need you. Rapids don't scare me. I'm keeping you around for insurance and 'cause you're good to look at."

They had awakened at dawn, though Muir beat him by several minutes. She thought long moments about creeping stealthily over the gear packed in mid-raft, and grabbing his gun before he could wake and fight for it.

The instant she made her decision and leaned toward him, her ever-so-slight movement brought him awake. He yawned, peeled eyes directly at her, wondering what she would have done if he'd stayed asleep.

"I'd tell you to rise and shine baby, but you're rowing, not rising. Get your cute tail on that plank and row your little heart out. Hard."

They'd moved swiftly down the current and now, an hour in to their journey, Muir straightened out the raft.

The empty beer can was crushed in Danny G's hands.

"You needed two hands for that?" Muir asked, though it wasn't really a question.

Danny G belched for answer.

"Good thinking by old River Rat to bring beer on his trips. Shame it gets dunk by a bunch of Japs and Eurocrappers."

He started to toss the can into the river--

"This river's got enough trash," Muir barked.

"What's that supposed to mean?"

"On the river, what we carry in, we carry out."

"I'll keep that in mind."

He tossed the can into the river. "Maybe."

Muir glowered as Danny G popped another beer and tossed the tab into the current--which seized it and swiftly carried it away. Up ahead they saw the first swifter thrust of current that signaled rapids.

They heard a roar.

"Welcome to the Colorado," Muir ironized.

The rapids came into view, dead ahead. The raft drifted toward them.

Danny G smirked: "Is this the life or what?"

She headed directly toward them, in the river's main flow. Danny G leaned back, lowered the gun. Smiled.

"Batten down those hatches, boys and girls."

Muir stood up to scout the passage ahead.

"There's boulders right and left. Our only chance is to make that chute in the middle.

Danny G smirked again, took a gulp of his beer.

"I don't feel like no bath today. Hit it, baby, counting on you."

She maneuvered the raft toward mid-current. The raging, wild rapids loomed.

Blake Wilson's 4x4 was leading the small caravan, among whom were the Starks, toward the Grand Canyon helicopter pad.

Blake was driving fast, and one of his passengers, the Senator, squirmed a bit. Blake said to him, "Our national parks make good hideouts. If someone's resourceful enough he can spend weeks passing himself off as a tourist or hiker. Maybe a lot longer."

"You've got your State Police, " the Senator countered.

"Yessir. But they're not stationed in the Park. It takes them time to get here and when they do...let's just say they need a good map. They're not equipped to head into the backcountry."

"Well, who's your local law enforcement?"

Blake didn't answer. The Congressman looked at Missy Martin. Skeptically.

She said, "We have our own police force, Senator. They perform a lot of enforcement duties."

"You ever used a gun?"

"No sir. Not even a bow and arrow. But they have."

"From time to time," Blake said. "The O.K. Corral, we are not."

The Senator nodded. Reassured, he wasn't.


Zane Bailey had halted in the South Rim pine forest to take a call from Blake. Today he'd been assigned to the

Zane protested, "You know how sound echoes off those canyon walls. He'll hear a chopper as soon as it gets down past the Esplanade."

"That's the idea. I'm going to rattle this guy."

"He's a psycho. Psychos are always rattled. Somebody's got to get down there and take him before he gets off the river."

"No way to do that, unless you're a bird."

This set Zane to thinking.

Blake continued, "Look, I've got people hustling to all the trailheads. Get down to Phantom Ranch, fast as you can go,. You've run down the South Kaibab in no time, and that's what I want today. In no time. Somebody's got to take care of those kids—"

"Harvey's the man for that. I've got another destination in mind. Trust me, sir. I'm going to get her back."

"Listen, you're not the goddamn Lone Ranger. Now—"

Blake heard a telltale click. His interlocutor had moved on. Whether to the South Kaibab or somewhere else remained TBD.

In the 4x4 Blake had no choice but to hang up too. He tossed the phone down, angry, and said to his passengers and anyone and everyone: "Never work with somebody who reminds you of yourself."


Muir's raft hit the roiling, foaming water, dipped, drew water, pitched up and down. Muir guided it expertly, but it was a battle.

Danny G let out a rebel yell as the raft plummeted into the deepest chute, spun like a cork, crested and seemed to hang suspended, then popped out...

Muir wrenched the oars, trying to right the raft. Did so.

They came hurtling out of the rapids. Danny G was soaked.

Muir relaxed, breathed easier.

Danny G noticed, "Shit, dropped my beer."

"There it is," Muir said. The can, not yet waterlogged, was zipping on the current.

"Swim after it. I'll wait for you."

"Yeah, sure. Hey, you and your hot little tail ever get tired of selling houses, this here's a real employment opportunity."

The caravan pulled up near the tarmac runway where the Canyon helicopters waited. Blake got out and headed over immediately to Josh Allen, who said, "Only two available. Lot of idiots getting overheated today."

"I just need one," Blake said. He turned to the Senator: "Wish it'd stayed a pleasure ride, Senator. Frankly, I'd feel better if you didn't come along. We'd planned a smooth over-flight of some spectacular Park scenery. This is going to be a hellride."

Josh added,"Wind currents get real bad when you fly low in the Canyon. You can't predict 'em and you can't control 'em."

"No sir," the Senator objected. "Chances are good we'll spot this lunatic and if we do, he's more likely to listen to a United States Senator. No disrespect intended."

"I appreciate your help," Blake responded.

"I've had a little more experience with this kind of flying," Josh said to Blake, though he knew what answer he'd get.

"You're the best. But she's my daughter."

Josh nodded, turned to get the copter revved. And seat the Senator.

Blake moved over to Pat and Richardson Stark. She was distraught.

"For the love of God Blake, get her back."

"I will. That's a promise."

She gave him a warmhearted, fervent hug that made Richardson a little uncomfortable despite the circumstances. But Blake was too worried for his daughter to care what Richardson thought. He turned past him and got into the helicopter.

Moments later it lifted off, with the Senator in the front passenger seat.

The raft had been pulled over to the bank just beyond the rapids they'd just run.

Danny G grabbed a six-pack, loaded it into his backpack and slung it over his shoulder.

"Bet you didn't think old Danny G knew about this trail. "Looks like we'll have it all to ourselves. No little runny nosed juvenile delinquents  singing Pop Goes the Weasel."

"I don't know anybody named Danny G. Or want to know."

"There you're wrong, baby. You ain't never heard rap like I can rap. Lyrics, beat, I got it all. World's gonna find that out some day, like after I shoot up a leftist Congressman's office. I got a song just for somebody like that, revolution song. Tell you what, I'll give you some samples while you're hiking. That is, if I can take my mind and other parts off that sweet buttered butt."

"This butt's staying here. I ran the river. So go do your thing, sing to the pumas and rattlers. They'll appreciate you more than me."

Danny G brandished his gun.

He whirled and abruptly fired off several bullets into the raft. Air whooshed out.

"You got about a minute before it sinks. Either you hit the trail or it takes you down with it. I ain't leaving a witness here working on her tan. *Capiche*?"

"This is called the Hartley Trail. It's a real gutbuster. From the looks of your gut, you're gonna get busted."

"That's why you're coming with. Push and pull, that's what you're gonna do if I get tired."

"You'll get tired, I guarantee it."

"Sounds to me like you know this trail. I got lucky choosing my guide."

She paused a moment, choosing her words.

"This doesn't make sense, you know. Going back up to the South Rim on the toughest trail in the Canyon. They'll be waiting for you. Rangers, police."

"Those rubes are gonna be prowling around the North Rim, as you damn well know. They're gonna be holding their tool in their hands while old Danny Boy parties with his friends. And hey, you're invited."

On the South Rim, his improvised corner of the earth for repairs and general maintenance, François was watching incredulously as Zane finished putting on his bird man suit.

"I don't understand. Why the Park Service check me out again? I got permit from Blake Wilson. Your litterbugs bigger problem than Bird Man."

"Have to make sure this thing's safe."

"Only way do that is to fly this thing. And you, no pilot, *non*?"

"Yeah." He took a deep breath. "You just hold your arms out and flap, right?"

"*Bien sur* no fucking way, idea is to catch wind and float on it, like glider. See, you—"

He held out his arms, showing him, then realized Zane had moved to the edge of the rim for what looked like a takeoff.

"If anything's damaged, the Park Service will reimburse you."

He leapt off into thin air.

"Oh *merde*...!" François yelled, "*putain de merde!*"

He rushed to the rim, looked over.

Zane was plunging like an anvil downward. No way was he "floating like bird." He was holding his arms out as François suggested, but the air was not catching. Terra firma from the South Rim was 5000 feet down, and it was closing fast. Zane waved his arms desperately, but the wings were not taking air.

Plummeting like one of the canyon's ancient boulders, he was rapidly approaching the Redwall set of cliffs. Just below, the thin sliver of green water that was the Colorado seen from the Rim was becoming a big roaring river.

Zane's face showed an increasing sense of desperation. Somewhere down there on the great river his Maker was waiting, and the first question he'd have to ask would be, Is Muir going to make it? It tore out his guts even before he'd crashed.

Up on the cliff François watched, beside himself, flapping his arms like an eagle. "Think like bird!" he screamed.

Apparently Zane wasn't. François could see him diving toward the cliffs looming directly ahead, gravity zooming him toward perdition.

But as François later said to all and sundry, especially those in the media, he could swear he suddenly heard the WHAPPP!!! of air suddenly hitting Zane's "wings," inflating his elbow pockets.

And instead of Zane splatting like a tomato against rock, the now bird-thinking Ranger leveled off with a WHOOSH and took flight, gliding over the cliffs and into the air over the next level of the Canyon where, below, lay the river.

François slumped to a sitting position on the cliff edge, weary with relief. He shook his head. *Heureusement,* this invention of François, she work so good.

He smiled to himself, couldn't help but think of a magic word, "Patent." And then another: "Rich."

But then another, more gnarly thought hit him.
"He didn't ask how to land!"


Zane was soaring now, caught in a good current.

He eyed the landscape ahead, got his bearings, angled his arms...and glided downward toward the river.

From a point of view near the Colorado, the lone flyer might well have been an object of beauty outlined against the spectacular green, red and ochre walls of the Canyon.

Soaring and gliding, Zane had come to a point high above the river where he could see for miles.

He looked long and far, trying to spot the raft with Muir and Danny G. But a strong Canyon wind current caught him, sent him spinning in the other direction. Zane struggled to right his trajectory. He dipped and spun down...


It had fallen to Dock to take the brood of inner-city kids in charge. Lee was trying to row. Though the raft was securely anchored, Dock had let out rope so that the raft could head into the current. Several other kids in the raft shouted encouragement. On the bank the rest of the kids waited their turn. The tourists watched, bemused.

"Y'all didn't come down to the Grand Canyon to sit on your behinds," Dock said.

"It's fun!" Lee agreed.

He managed to back the raft out of the lee eddy and into the current. Sitting beside him, Dock said he was impressed.

"Ok, left arm back row."

Lee managed to do it and the raft righted, merged with the current.

"Bravo!" Dock said.

BING!

Like an animal on a leash, the raft hit the end of its tether.

"Aw, can't we go on?" Lee asked.

"Not unless you've got a couple thousand dollars. My time is money and you already owe me 10 bucks."

"10 bucks!"

"Hey, if you manage to row us back against the current, I'll forgive your debt."

Lee tried, battling, but the raft barely moved. He struggled with as much of his strength as he could gather.

"Rowing against the current," Dock said. "It's always tough, and in rapids, impossible. One thing you've got to remember if you look at the river like life, and I do: make sure you know which way the current flows. It'll make your days a lot easier."

Adding wryly: "Or else...find a partner who's got a lot of elbow grease."

Dock slid over and took the oars and managed to wheel the raft back to its moorings.

Lee had to endure both praise and catcalls, but he enjoyed both.

"I wish Miss Muir had stayed around to see me. Why couldn't she stay around?"

"Well Lee, I can tell you for sure, she wouldn't have gone off for no reason. I'd say it was pretty important and it wasn't something you all needed to know about. She was protecting you. Anyway, you're in good hands with John and those trusty Grand Canyon mules."

"Maybe she'll be waiting for us at the top."

Luckily the other kids gathered around Lee and Dock didn't have to answer the question. He gestured to his passengers and they began piling back into the rafts.

Dock welcomed back his boaters with a jolly quiz question:

"Yesterday we saw near a dozen eagles. You see any yet, folks?"

Lee wasn't done and he yelled, "I see one!"

An eagle of sorts. As all eagerly peered upward, what they saw was Zane Bailey, plunging down toward a landing...also of sorts. He was aiming for the beach where the tourists and rest of the rafting party were, but the Canyon downdrafts were playing hell with him.

Dock corrected, "Folks, that is not your basic eagle."

Two Japanese tourists in Dock's party began busily snapping pictures as the erstwhile Bird Man headed down.

They all watched wide-eyed as Zane approached, flapping his wings to alter trajectory and avoid the cliff edge...just managing to lurch over it and then--

Down toward the water. Where he hit with a giant SPLASH and disappeared.

Dock hopped over, took an oar and hurriedly rowed over to where Zane went under.

For what seemed very long moments, no one saw movement.

Dock anxiously scanned downstream for signs of life...

Zane popped up to the surface next to him, spitting water.

Dock stretched out an oar. Zane grabbed it. Looked up at the rafting party. All the kids who'd rushed to the bank to watch were staring at him, open-mouthed.

Dock said, "Boy, you're no advertisement for manned wing flight. What took you so long to come up?"

Zane was breathless but managed to say, "Getting undressed."

He took a deep breath: "I need a kayak."

A short time later, under time pressure, Zane was getting into one of Dock's kayaks. Dock stood beside with a paddle, handed it to him when he was well situated in the boat.

All the others--kids, Dock's rafting party and tourists snapping pictures--watched.

Dock warned, "If you're thinking of running those Class 5 & 6 rapids in this thing, you're gonna miss your funeral."

"You did it once."

"Yeah, but I was younger then—and drunk!"

Zane paddled off.

## One-man Cavalry

Blake Wilson's chopper was being buffeted by Canyon up- and downdrafts. Both men inside were grateful for their seatbelts. Blake shouted into his headset mike to the Senator:

"Cell phones don't work well in the Canyon. Too many high walls, they'll just send the signal bouncing around. You don't lock on to a satellite, you'll be talking to your echo."

They hit a big bump, bounced...

The Senator did not look good. Each jolt, each air pocket made him look worse. Scanning the canyon below for signs of Danny G and Muir, Blake did not remark the increasing discomfort of his distinguished passenger. But as the queasiness visibly mounted on the Senator's visage--

"Pretty smooth ride so far," Blake assured him.

This was too much for the Senator. If this was what they called a "smooth ride"...

He leaned down and vomited onto the floor.

In the kayak, Zane came upon the first set of rapids run by Muir. He paddled hard—toward the rapids directly ahead.

He hit the chute directly, bounced—flipped.

The water zipped the kayak pellmell, and Zane stayed under. But when he hit smooth water, he rolled rightside up. Without missing a beat, or in his case, paddle stroke, he continued downriver.

"So far so good," he said to himself, "and one good thing about these rapids—they give me a hell of a push. Kinetic energy taking me to Muir Wilson. I'll catch up to them if they haven't taken out."

It occurred to him, because he wasn't born yesterday, that Danny G might not leave a raft behind to signal the takeout point.

"But then again, he might. He won't be expecting pursuit so soon. Roll on, big river."

He paddled hard. Really hard.


Zane hit the chute head on. Whitewater surrounded him, pounding the kayak. Nothing to do but go with it. Zane flipped, righted himself. Another wall of water loomed ahead, this one immense. The little kayak hit it and went under.

This time Zane did not come up.


The helicopter was heading over the rapids. Blake peered down.

Motioned to the Senator.

"We're going down!"

Blake sent the chopper careening down. Wind drafts pounded the aircraft like a bird feather.

The Senator was in agony.

They flew over the rapids. If Blake had known these were the rapids where one of his erstwhile Rangers had just gone down, he would have lingered.

But looking hard, he saw nothing but whitewater.

He motioned to the Senator. The helicopter rapidly ascended, flew on.


Down below, the kayak broke the surface...but there was still no sign of Zane.

The kayak was tossed willy-nilly by the raging whitewater, Zane nowhere to be seen in the roiling foam...

Underwater he was struggling to gain some control as he hurtled along in the current.

He hit an object...the submerged raft.

A shot of adrenalin kicked in.

Zane rose to the surface, spitting water. He headed for shore, battling current—reached the river bank downstream of the trail he recognized.

He'd have to work hard to get back to that trailhead, battling the river. But a miracle had just happened and he saw no reason why a second one couldn't follow. He was going to do his damndest, and whoever sent miracles earth's way he felt sure would recognize that.

Danny G and Muir were making their way up the trail when they heard the helicopter.

Muir seized the chance to run away, sliding down the slope to where she could signal the chopper.

Danny G slid down the slope after her, tackled her. She cried out, hurt by the force, but quickly recovered. She was strong and managed to twist over onto her back and get a clear shot at DG's jaw. She belted him.

He lurched back, stunned by the force of her punch.

Muir squirmed out from under him and headed down the trail. She made good time but just before rounding a curve a gunshot ricocheted off the rock beside her head...just missing her.

"Next one takes your head off, bitch!" Danny G yelled.

The shot had stopped her in her tracks.

"Now get your ass back up here, and fast!"

Muir had no choice but to do it. She could hear the helicopter approaching closer.

"Faster!" he screamed.

She put vim in her step but not 100%, thinking, if he only knew how fast I could run up this trail, even the Hartley. She'd done an out and back rim-to-rim marathon once.

But she saw no reason to tell him that.

Danny G grabbed Muir, shoved her under cover of a rock and tamarisk tree just before the plane came into view. He put gun to her head.

Blake and the Senator peered hard but passed over the hiding place of Muir and Danny G without spotting them.

The chopper banked and continued downriver.

Muir looked distressed, her face twisted in a grimace of pain as Danny G shoved it against the rock.

"You are one macho bull dyke. Damn near broke my jaw. It hurts. Gets to hurting too much, I'll take you out. You understand me?"

She nodded, still grimacing. He let go.

He shoved her forward. "Get your ass in gear."

Downriver, Blake saw nothing but river and rapids, no sign of people. He signaled to the Senator and they headed away from the river, toward the North Rim.

Zane was wringing out his wet shirt. He put it back on. In this canyon desert it would dry in no time He rolled up his pants legs into shorts. The tracks of Danny G and Muir were apparent in the dirt.

The Hartley Trail wasn't made for runners, and he wouldn't be able to run at a steady rhythm.

"But I'm going to damn well try," he told himself.

## Business as Usual

The Visitor Centers on both Grand Canyon rims bustle from opening hour to closing. On the South Rim, open all year, about the only time onsite Rangers have to themselves, sans visitors, is when a blizzard has clogged entrance roads to the park. But even then, some people straggle in, knocking snow off their boots and parkas. Somebody, some time, will have to mop up the water in their wake.

That somebody would be the aforesaid Rangers, adding mop duty to their myriad others. Very few, it has to be said, of the thousands and thousands of visitors who pass through every year truly and thoroughly appreciate what and how well those duties are fulfilled, in all times and temperatures and nationalities and challenges of one kind or other.

Perhaps that was one reason Acting Chief Ranger Raymond Gunther entered the South Rim Visitor Center with Joe Blevins in tow.

He eyed the band of visitors who already crowded in to the Center but continued marching vigorously, as always, toward the main counter where young Rangers Diana Harper and Rex Richardson were dealing with any and all comers.

"How we doing, troops?"

"Same old same old, except it's a new day and we're still new."

"Like me," Raymond said, smiling. "Mr. Joe Blevins here has been through a lot the last few days and I thought the best way for him to recuperate was to make a little film about what we do here at the Visitor Center."

Blevins said, "I've got a blog and you might say I'm a pretty serious Influencer. Thousands of followers. Acting Chief Gunther's lent me a National Park Service phone and I'm raring to go."

"If you two agree," Raymond qualified to the Rangers. "No stars are born around here without their permission."

Rex said, "I'm ready for my closeup."

Diana added, "If I'd known you were coming, Mr. Blevins, I'd have worn makeup."

"Which she knows is not permitted here," Raymond joshed. "We go natural, like this great park."

"That's the kind of quotes I'm looking for," Joe said excitedly as Acting Chief Gunther handed him the cellphone.

"An hour ought to be sufficient," Raymond said. "We don't want to wear out Rex and Diana."

"Absolutely, Chief," Joe agreed, "I'm your biggest fan."

Joe Blevins began organizing his shoot. Diana said sotto voce to Raymond, "I kind of thought the Austrian couple would be more traumatized than him."

"Nope," Raymond said, "they're dayhiking a ways down the South Kaibab. Mr. Blevins asked for a psychologist but I said, we practice psychology every day here."

"Glad to see you here, sir," said Becky Harrell, another member of the Center crew this day who'd just left off advising a family of six. "Glad you're the one holding the fort. How terrible for Chief Wilson. His daughter kidnapped when he's not even one week on the job."

"One week or a thousand, he'd feel the same distress, Becky. He's going to get her back, I promise you. Actually we're counting on you all to hold the fort. Make it business as usual, like it's supposed to be. No alarm, no freak outs. We've got jobs to do."

Diana said firmly, "We've got this, Chief."

She noticed now that Joe Blevins had filmed her comment. He spoke for the camera and his eventual followers, "That's the spirit these Rangers display each and every minute, good people out there. I Joe Blevins am deeply proud that my tax dollars are funding them."

Raymond Gunther signaled to his troops that he had to be on his way and was, off to coordinate a typical day at the park, except this day with a manhunt in progress.

Joe Blevins found as he circulated with his camera that as he often observed, people of all walks of life and nationalities were eager to talk.

But first: "Where's the restroom please?" asked a woman with a strong accent that Joe recognized as indigenous to his native Texas.

Rex pointed to a sign on the nearby wall. "Right that way, m'am, just down the hall."

The woman had several fairly unruly kids in tow and her husband, if present, was not in proximity at this point in time.

"Not much of a sign," she complained, miffed a bit that she hadn't spotted it before.

"Yes m'am, we try to make trail and park signs discreet. Kind of a national park philosophy."

"Not much of a sign," she grumbled again as she directed herself and brood toward the restrooms.

Joe Blevins turned his camera on Rex.

"That happen often?"

"All the time. Let me say for your followers, we keep our restrooms clean and sanitary at all times. It's part of our job and we're committed to doing it."

"Bravo," Joe seconded.

He spent some time filming the visitors who queued up to the main counter, usually to pose questions regarding trails and other information.

Diana passed a lot of time, he noticed, repeating facts about main trails off the rim, and emphasizing politely and over and over how important it was to take water and mind the heat and temperature.

"It gets awful hot the lower down you go," she said numerous times, "so be aware of your limits. Don't push yourself too hard. Take lots of water. It's springtime but don't be fooled by the temps in the morning. By afternoon you'll be doing a lot of sweating."

One of the men to whom she expostulated listened, or seemed to listen, to her polite spiel, took the brochure she handed to him, then moved over to speak to Joe and his camera. "Going down the South Kaibab," he said. "Jim Churley, that's me. You can follow me on Twitter, I'm doing a blow by blow."

Joe noticed Jim's footwear.

"Those sandals look a little fragile, Jim."

"Back home I hike barefoot. Believe it or not, it's true. These trails are a walk in the park."

"Well, the Rangers—"

"They've got to cover their butts, public servants and all. Avoid lawsuits. Here I go, boys and girls, follow me on Twitter."

Joe turned his viewer on himself and said to his fans, "There you go, a macho guy who doesn't believe in what the Rangers say. That's the kind of frustration they have to deal with every day, folks who don't listen. Just about every day they have to send off a rescue team to bring back some hiker who's exhausted or dehydrated. Isn't that right, Ranger Becky Harrell?"

Becky took center stage of Blevins' camera.

"Unfortunately that's true," she answered. "It's absolutely important to respect the warning signs we've stationed on the trails and even overlooks. Sometimes it's really really difficult to get access to a person in distress. It's a wilderness out there and just to get a stretcher up and down can get to be a real challenge."

"Some people don't make it, isn't that right?" Joe asked.

"That's an unfortunate fact."

"There's a lesson here, folks," Joe commented, "and Ranger Harrell can't emphasize it enough. Obey those signs! Thank you so much, Ranger Harrell."

"You're welcome."

He followed her as she turned to a man who'd been waiting impatiently.

"I'd like to camp here tonight, recharge my van and everything," he said. "Internet won't let me get a reservation. You talk about lame software. You people need to upgrade. So we don't have to come here and spend time in person."

"Sir, the campgrounds here fill up months in advance. If you don't find an opening, well, it means we don't have an opening."

"You're kidding me. Everybody knows it's like a restaurant, you keep some tables open for VIPs. I can tell you who I am but you probably recognize me."

"I'm sorry, I don't. I don't watch too much TV."

"Yeah, nature girl. Anyway, tell me what you can do for me."

"We can put you on a waiting list, but if I understand, you've got an RV—"

"Deluxe. You should come see it, you'll want this kind of vehicle in your campground."

"We don't have RV hookups."

"You've got to be kidding me."

"But I can direct you to Trailer Village—"

Blevins turned away from the duo and headed toward the Center Museum. "Let's leave this VIP, or at least VIP in his own mind, and enter the museum which has many useful exhibits for visitors to learn about the flora and fauna."

The camera made a slow tour of the above, with occasional commentary by Joe Blevins and the visitors who were strolling through. Blevins held for a moment on a boy of about 10 who stared agog at a glass-enclosed exhibit of a puma, a lifelike model that almost seemed real.

"Look at his eyes, Dad," the boy said. "He looks real mean. He could just tear up our dog."

"And us too," his father agreed.

"What do we do if we run into one?"

Joe Blevins entered the conversation.

"That happens very rarely," he interjected. "I studied up before coming here. They're nocturnal animals. Unless you roam around in the wilderness at night, you won't encounter a puma. Or cougar, some call them. They're the same creature, you know."

"But what if you do?" the boy asked.

"Yeah," his father seconded.

"Well, from my research, if you bang on a pot or pan or make loud screeching noises of one kind or another, they turn tail. Me, I always hang a big metal drinking cup on my belt, for just such an eventuality. Rare as it is."

"That's good advice. Thank you, sir. He's filming, Tommy. Thank the gentleman."

"Thank you, Mister," Tommy said to the Influencer.

"Have a great trip and don't forget to thank the National Park Service Rangers before you go, okay? For all the work they do."

Joe Blevins' allotted shoot time was nearing an end and he filmed a selfie denouement:

"That's it for now, you guys. I've been here an hour and just listening to people and their questions questions questions, I've got to say I'm beat. And I haven't even been working. How these dedicated public servants do their jobs so well and with such courtesy just surpasses all my comprehension. Let's send them a collective shout-out.

"And while we're at it, let's give a special thought to those Rangers handling the kidnap situation I explained in my last posts. The kidnapper hasn't just stolen my phone, he's taken a hostage and Chief Blake Wilson has taken charge of the manhunt in more ways than one.

"For all of them I say, and for all of us, in the words of the great Theodore Roosevelt, 'Bully! Keep making us proud, ladies and gentlemen.'"

And with that, Joe Blevins signed off.

## Hood's Western Marshals

Marshall Hood's Freedom Town compound lay squarely in the Arizona Strip, the isolated region to the east of Las Vegas, north of the Grand Canyon and generally, as Hood liked to claim, "a long way from anywhere. That's the way patriots like it when they prepare for a liberation crusade."

Blake Wilson saw the complex of prefab buildings and tents and soldier training grounds a good while before arriving. The land here was wide and wide open, which ordinarily would pose a problem in defending against attacks, but getting here required an aircraft or a land expedition—it was that remote.

Hood liked to say, "No services here for you motorists, unless you wear your badge of freedom and carry a contribution to the cause of righteous conflict."

The Senator wondered, "They going to welcome us with some artillery, Blake? You let them know a US Senator is on board?"

"Didn't have time, sir. But they haven't crossed over into armed rebellion. Yet."

The chopper came in for a landing on the hard gravel runway laid across the desert by Hood's paramilitary boys.

It set down in front of a formidable military tank, barrel pointed directly at it and any other invading aircraft that might not be considered friendly. The tank made an impression on the Senator as he climbed out.

Men in camouflage fatigues with assault weapons formed a double file, a sort of gauntlet for the visitors to walk through to reach the door of the bunker-like building where

Marshall Hood waited. Gun strapped to his waist, in military khaki and cap, he resembled the officer he wanted to be.

The rifles carried by the flanking "troops" were cocked. The Senator looked a little nervous.

"What's with these people. They act like we're the enemy."

"We are, sir. We're the government."

They reached Hood.

Blake said,

"Marshall Hood. You recognize the Senator?"

"I surely do," Hood said. He thrust out his hand. "Appreciated your vote on that gun control legislation. You did our country a great service."

The Senator replied, "I'm against any law that unnecessarily restricts our freedoms, but I have to tell you frankly Mr. Hood, I don't approve of militia groups."

"Hood's Western Marshals is an organization of patriots. No more, no less."

Blake rejoindered, "Some of your so-called patriots have criminal records as long as their arms."

"I believe in second chances. The USA was built on that principle. Senator, I'd like to invite you to a drink of whiskey. All-American pure gut-buster, brewed 100 per cent in the American South."

He turned to Blake. "You're welcome to my hospitality, too."

Blake countered sharply, "We haven't come to drink aperitifs. We're looking for Danny G Grissom. There's only one reason he's crossing the Canyon. To join you."

Hood commented directly to the Senator: "The Park Service—and I use that word service sarcastically—is always looking to blame me. Every chipmunk steals a camper's piece of sugar, he says it's Marshall Hood and his boys. I never heard of this what's his name. What'd he do, uproot a cactus?"

Blake suddenly grabbed his throat, shoved him against the wall of the bunker. Hood's men reacted, cocking rifles, pointing them at Blake.

"He's got my daughter. You hear me? My daughter!"

The men hesitated. The Senator freaked. Hood raised his arm for his men to desist.

Blake spat out, "Get a message to him. He touches her, you'll get your war all right. But not with these toy soldiers. It'll be you and me, man to man. Then we'll see how tough you are."

He let go of him, stalked away. Hood choked, put arm to throat.

"You see that, Senator? That's what they call a civil servant. We could take him out right now in legitimate self-defense, if we were the crazy gun nuts people say."

The Senator gave a half-smile. "I didn't see any assault. Just an anxious father delivering a message. If I were you I'd pass it on."

He headed away after Blake. Hood rubbed his throat, thinking. Angry. He looked at his men.

"Buster…Jimbo."

Two of the paramilitaries stepped forward. Both looked like they could wrestle a tank.

"He's too public. The Western Marshals are gonna do a job the State Police and Park Rangers can't. People are gonna fall all over themselves thanking us. Even some stupid politicians. Take him out and do it right, you hear what I'm saying? Before he can say 'hello.' "

The aptly named Buster asked, "What about the girl?"

"She happens to get in the line of fire, it'll be a tragedy for Blake Wilson. But we citizens'll have a safer national park, won't we?"

## Closing In

Danny G and Muir were switchbacking up the trail, so rough and shaly and rocky that every step was a battle not to slide back down. Danny G was sweating, panting, signaled to her in the lead to stop. He gasped for air.

"Want me to call that chopper?" Muir said. "Jail's more comfy and easier on the lungs. Pretty soon you're going to be sweating blood. I've seen it happen, trust me. And then your heart explodes."

"I ain't got no heart, baby."

He looked up at where they were heading.

"Old Mr. Hartley must have been the dumbest ass hermit ever came to this canyon. His trail makes the goats puke."

"The view makes it all worth it."

"Like I got the energy to look. You got a boy friend?"

"No. Not that it's any of your business."

"That's a crock. A hot buttered bunny like you…"

"The Grand Canyon's better for scenery than eligible men."

"Looked to me like Ranger Rick's carrying a torch for you. The way his eyes turned green when he saw me sweet talking you. If he'd had a shotgun I'd be mounted on his truck right now."

"He didn't like you interrupting his lecture. He hates me."

"I'm not crazy fond of you myself. Way you've had that nose all turned up, like I was a skunk or something."

He raised her chin up with his palm, forced her to look at him. She tried not to flinch or show revulsion.

"But I like how you look in those shorts…sweated off that expensive makeup, too. Now you look real, not like some phony real estate hustler."

Muir said defiantly, "You know what? It's another couple of hours to the Rim. If I'm going to have to hear bullshit like that, I'd rather you shoot me."

He seemed taken aback by her boldness, didn't know at first how to respond.

"You got *cojones*. With a capital C. Naw. When we get to the top, you're going to give me a little pick-me-up."

He motioned to her to move on. They started back up the trail.

Harvey Pine hiked swiftly—Zane Bailey was the only Ranger on staff who could move faster—and the only reason he had never done an Iron Man feat of running rim to rim and back was, he had a tendency to stop and give numerous counsels to those not respecting trail regulations. And as well, those who did.

This day however he had speed as a priority and he ran swiftly down the South Kaibab trail. It was steep, a veritable knee-knocker for most anyone, but he was motivated even more than usual and he encountered the mule train ferrying the city kids back up to the South Rim before it had even reached the halfway point.

"Hi there, boys and girls!" he announced, scarcely breathing hard. After they'd voiced multiple hi's and hello's, he explained, "Thought I'd walk with you today. That all right?"

Lee and the others seconded the notion.

"You just got down. Now you've got to go back up," Lee observed.

"Well, think of this trail as an up and down escalator," Harvey responded, "except unlike an escalator, here you've got to use your feet."

Lee nodded, wondering if there was another meaning to this statement besides the obvious.

Harvey lowered his voice and asked a question for John's ears only: "Any trauma situations here?"

"Not that I can see. You might say, they've come from situations where they see traumas every day."

"Right. Good observation. But let's don't take anything for granted. Ok, boys and girls. And John. And all you mules too. Upward and onward!"

John smiled, gently kicked his mule and the train got on the move. Harvey fell in step, started with Lee and then moved down alongside the riders one by one, quizzing.

"How are you doing today, young man?"

"I'm ok, sir."

"Call me Harvey. Harvey Pine, like the tree. Except you'll notice we don't see a lot of pine trees here. Why do you think that is?"

Lee didn't have to reflect.

"It's not flat."

"You're partly right, it's steep and rocky with a vertical dropoff, but let me tell you, these Canyon pines can take root in the darnedest places. I'll show you some on the way up. Would you like that?"

"Cool!"


Hustling up the trail at a fast pace, Zane came up short. A telltale buzzing told him in advance what he now saw, a rattlesnake blocking the trail, coiled to strike, its tongue darting out as if just craving to taste flesh, i.e., his.

It looked mean and was poised to attack at Zane's least move forward.

Zane looked...no way around. The trail went up and was sheer on one side—the other. And no branch stick lying around on the ground to use as a prod.

"Move on. Go back to your hole. I've got business and no time to negotiate."

The snake rattled viciously.

"I'm coming through, pardner. One way or another."

More rattling. The trail skirted a sheer dropoff on one side and on the other, thick brush ideal for snakes but not men and he'd have to fight his way through. If his newfound enemy seized a moment of entanglement, he would stay tangled.

"Guess it's another," Zane grimaced.

He wrapped his shirt around his wrist and forearm. Took a deep breath. Thrust it forward. The snake struck.

Zane winced. Pulled back. The snake was still angry, immovable. Zane thrust again and again the fangs stuck.

Now the snake had enough. Its venom virtually exhausted, it was harmless.

Zane hurried past. The snake made no move to strike.

Moments later Zane stopped to unwrap the shirt and inspect his wound. Two fang marks were visible on his forearm.

He looked back at the snake crawling away.

"Not too deep but I'm going to be sick...let's hope not too bad."

He headed up the trail.


Further up the trail, Danny G and Muir rounded a crest. Behind them they saw a magnificent panorama.

But Danny G didn't care. He had his attention firmly fixed on Muir's legs.

He found the breath to gasp, "You work out, honey bunch?"

"Started the day I came out of the womb."

DG found enough wind to say, "Paid off."

He looked upward at the trail ahead. "How much farther we got to go on this sucker? And don't give me any bullshit."

"About four miles. Tough miles. You want to call it quits, a helicopter can land at Panorama Point. You can admire the view and wait for transportation. And then three squares a day, courtesy of US taxpayers."

"Aren't you the big joker. I'd fall down laughing except this ain't the place to fall down. Unless it's on you. Sounds like Panorama Point's got some flat ground, and where there's flat ground, people can get to business perpetuating the species. Understand what I'm saying, honey bunch?"

"Two words. Fuck you."

He grinned. "Well, if you insist. Let's get going to that Panorama Point."

Just this moment Zane Bailey was vomiting his guts out...reacting to the snake venom in his system. He looked ravaged, struggled to stay upright. He was hunched over against a rock, teetering on the edge of a precipice. Nevertheless he straightened up.

"No rattler's going to put me down," he thought to himself, and then said out loud to the wind and sun and whoever might hear him on the trail ahead: "The Cavalry's coming, Muir!"

He painfully lurched upward, struggling but advancing one footstep at a time, undaunted.

# Vigilantes

Buster and Jimbo's destination lay not so very far away as the crow flies, but they weren't crows, and their 4x4 couldn't fly either.

"We got to haul ass," Jimbo said to his partner in crime—literally—and they roared away from Hood's compound with just some spare water, a few Snickers bars for sustenance, and the tools they needed for the job at hand. Whether it came to taking down Danny G at long range or close up, they had the equipment, neither begged nor borrowed but definitely stolen from US forces of law and order.

The boys had been convinced by Marshal Hood that they were and in the near future would be said forces, and they'd bought in to his philosophy, policies and methods. They hadn't needed much convincing, in truth. They'd left the straight and narrow hardly after teething.

"Yeah, keep reminding me," Buster agreed, already giving an excellent imitation of hauling ass. The roads leading away from the Arizona Strip and down toward the canyon were long and unfrequented and one could practice for the Indianapolis 500 without pesky state troopers to hinder and just the occasional private vehicle, its driver usually quite nervous traversing the wide open and empty spaces that put fear in those contemporary citizens who'd long ago left pioneer attitudes and gumption far behind.

Buster was driving like a bat out of hell, not caring if he forced any of these stray vehicles off the road--which from time to time, he did. He and Jimbo had miles to go before they slept, and a quarry who had a date with death.

The Mercedes moved slowly on the road back to Grand Canyon Village. Richardson Stark had no desire to go back to work. He had other ideas in mind.

Neither he nor Pat had had much to say when Blake Wilson brought the helicopter to a landing for refueling.

Desperate for news, they'd heard nothing.

"What's the plan, Blake?" his ex-wife had asked, plaintively. "You must have a plan, yes?"

"Keep looking," he said grimly. "They can't stay hidden forever."

"That a fact or a hope?" Richardson had followed up.

When Blake Wilson took a call in lieu of answering, Richardson Stark drew his conclusions.

"He takes a United States Senator along but can't find room for us. For God's sake, we're family. We've got eyes and we're not going to be rehearsing what we're going to say to frigging reporters. "

Pat said, "I know you want to do all you can. But where they may have to take that little helicopter...if something should happen and then Muir too—" She choked, struggled to talk. "I couldn't bear it. No dear, this is one time all your money and influence can't do a thing. Blake knows this Canyon a lot better than we do. We just have to wait."

Richardson disagreed, said angrily, "Money always talks. If I offer a million bills, even a psychopath will listen."

He pulled the Mercedes to a stop in front of the hangar that housed Russ McGuiness' helicopters. Only one remained, the others being out in the skies, ferrying tourists on sightseeing flights.

All this was explained to Richardson by young Jimmy Jones, holding the fort in Russ' absence. Richardson saw his chance and launched into a serious negotiation.

"The card's right here in your hands. You're an experienced pilot, right?"

"Yes sir. I can take that thing anywhere and Mr. McGuiness knows it. But well, he's the boss."

"Send him a text. You're going to be taking customers paying ten times your usual flight fee. He'll wet his pants."

"Mr. McGuiness? I doubt that, sir."

"Just an expression, son. And just between us, you do your job and take us where we want to go, let's just say your tip will exceed your salary."

Jimmy's eyes lit up. This time as often, money did indeed talk.


Russ McGuiness didn't respond to Jimmy's text because one, he was piloting tourists from England toward the Deer Falls and Thunder River area, and second, he'd spotted a pair of hikers.

He picked up his cell and called Blake Wilson.

"Couldn't make them out but it looked like a man and woman. These eyes of mine aren't infallible but I could swear they weren't carrying packs. Who takes the Hartley on an out and back without a pack?"

"Iron men or folks who think they are, but I'll check out the backcountry registers. Thanks, Russ."

"You take care now."

"Not at a time like this."

Blake put in a call to Lucinda, now back at the Backcountry Office, and it didn't take long for her to give a response: "Nobody signed up for the Hartley, chief."


When Buster and Jimbo arrived at the South Rim entrance station, they had a surprise waiting for them.

"Pay? We got to pay at one of our national parks?" Buster asked.

"Since when's this been going on?" Jimbo wondered, genuinely.

"Sounds like this is your first experience at one of our said national parks. You boys sound like Americans born and bred. So you're taxpayers."

"Yeah, we pay for this place," Buster complained.

"And without these entrance fees, I'm afraid you'd pay a heck of a lot more taxes.  Our foreign visitors come in big numbers but not quite enough to offset fees for upkeep and maintenance and law enforcement."

This last put the quietus on the two disciples of Marshal Hood. They couldn't be sure it was meant for them, but Jimbo said later that he hadn't liked the way the Ranger at the Entrance Station looked at him.

"Old doofus shoulda retired. You see how he couldn't handle us paying in cash?"

In fact Clarence Hillis had hinted more than once that he'd prefer they pay with a credit card. Not because he liked plastic. For ID reasons.

"Hell, we don't got enough left to buy a coke," Buster grimaced.

"We've got real spring water at our drinking fountains," Clarence smiled. He handed them the customary Grand Canyon brochures.

"Enjoy your stay," he said.

Jimbo said, "Thank you, sir. You've been real courteous and we appreciate that. Can't wait to see that Canyon."

He nodded to Buster and they headed into the park.

"What the hell was that?" Buster asked his colleague. "Talked to him like he was your longlost Daddy."

"Might have been. My Daddy was gone before I even came out of my Mama's pouch. No, you dumb fuck. You made us conspicuous. I was talking like all these foreign trash who pay our bills, yeah right old man."

"Anyway," Buster said, "whatever. He ain't gonna remember us any more'n his old lady's name. Guy should be out to pasture, gettin' his Alzheimer's treated."

But Clarence Hillis didn't have to remember too much because he'd made sure to note the boys' license plate.

He phoned it in to Lincoln Williams. "

"You're sure they're Hood's men?" Lincoln asked.

"If they're not, he's missing out on two Neanderthals."

"I'll get a watch on them. Hey, thanks for stepping in. You didn't have to, you know."

Clarence chuckled—even as he welcomed and took the entrance fee from the next motorist.

"Hey, it was either this or do greeter duty at Wal-Mart. Extra cash. They tell me electric rocking chairs cost some bucks." Clarence added: "If those goons are prowling around on the South Rim, it means something. I can guarantee you they didn't come prepared for a hike. Wish I'd checked their trunk."

"And get yourself sent to the Promised Land? No, you've got some rocking to do before then. You put me in this job for a reason, right? And you were right. I've got a feeling these boys came from a neighborhood just like mine."

## Showdown at Panorama Point

Danny G and Muir saw Russ McGuiness' chopper head off toward the North.

"It's a frigging freeway here."

"We call it the Dragon Corridor. Tourist flights. All day every day, weather permitting."

Muir searched the skies for another aircraft. Danny G smirked.

"You thinking of signaling? Hey, rip off that shirt. That'll get some attention, I guarantee you. Starting first with your old buddy Danny G."

"Rap on. Like usual, nobody's come to listen."

Danny G turned sour. They had reached Panorama Point after a grueling ascent where she'd hoped her captor would collapse with fatigue or any sort of cardiac crisis that would put him down. But as much as he suffered, he kept ascending. And most unfortunately, did not let fall his gun.

At Panorama Point he'd signaled another rest stop. She'd moved out onto the rock shelf that overlooked the incredible panorama of canyon. On her trip when she'd met Zane they had both agreed it was the most spectacular viewpoint in the entire Grand Canyon. It was the only thing they'd agreed on, then or since.

She wondered if the news of her kidnapping had reached him, and whether he'd care very much more than if she'd been any random tourist. Probably he would be happy that one less house sale would go down today.

Danny G had gotten his wind back, enough to leer. His quip had given birth to a thought, and worse, desire.

He moved over, rubbed his body against her seductively.

"You give me what I want, I'll be real nice to you. I may even let you go."

She flinched back, repulsed.

He spat, "What's the matter, you don't like cowboys? We've been gettin' along real good."

"You want to play, play with the only person who likes you. Yourself."

He hit her hard across the face with his gun, drawing blood.

She spat out, "You need a gun to take me, you pussy?"

He hit her again, and this time the blow knocked her to the ground, half unconscious.

He threw himself on her, grabbing her arms.

"Asleep or awake, don't matter to me."

He leaned on her, grabbed her by the hair till she screamed, hit her again. She had to remain motionless. He bent over to kiss her—

"HEY! HEY!"

The sound of another man's voice echoing off the canyon walls startled Danny G. Was he dreaming?

"Let her go, you gutless fuck!" yelled the voice, enraged.

Danny stood up and looked in the direction of a voice he now realized was not a dream but very, very real—from Zane Bailey, rushing up the Hartley toward him.

"Well well well, look who's here."

He moved away to the ledge, the better to see the Ranger who was now running their way.

"Come on, boy, join the party!" he yelled to Zane.

Muir struggled to her feet.

Danny G said to her, "Like old Snow White, your prince is coming. The goddamn idiot. Some brave stupid hoss."

"Go back, Zane! He'll kill you!"

In the flash of a glance, watching Zane hurry toward them, thoughts crashed into Muir's mind and heart: first, that she loved him. He'd broken every rule in the book to get here like this, not to mention those involving good sense, but she knew he'd done it because he loved her.

Second, that it was just like him to get himself killed just when they'd broken through the mundane barriers separating them and could have had a life together.

And third, she could not bear to see him killed, right there in front of her. Which was going to happen.

Danny G seemed to read her thoughts: "Yeah, old Prince C's not gonna make it to the altar."

Zane reached Panorama Point and confronted them. He saw the blood and bruise on Muir's face.

"Some brave shithead, beating up on a girl," he said contemptuously to Danny G, who grinned and countered, "I'd beat up on you, 'cept you wouldn't put up much of a tussle with a bullet in your gut. Which you're gonna get."

Zane moved slowly toward him.

"As you want. But let her go."

"Go where? This here's the wilderness, hoss. Some Ranger you are."

"I'm not leaving you," Muir said with force.

"Aw, now ain't that lovey-dovey. Stop right there."

Danny G brandished the gun, pointed it at Zane a few paces away.

"You thinking of rushing me, go right ahead. I won't even have to aim."

The sound of a helicopter intruded. Unlike the constant hum of sightseeing planes and choppers, this one was close and getting closer.

They looked, saw it roaring their way, coming fast as the aircraft could go.

"That's the cavalry," Zane said. "Give it up. Game's over."

"Not on your life. Literally."

"In that case, I've got nothing to lose."

To Muir's horror and Danny G's surprise, Zane came running pell-mell toward the gunman, who had time to fire off a shot before Zane tackled him.

They fell together onto the rock. Zane disengaged enough to punch Danny G once, twice, then over and over, blows reduced in force because the Ranger had to use one arm to pinion Danny G's gun hand.

And then, the blood flowing from his gunshot wound took a toll. Zane weakened and Danny G gained an upper hand. He punched Zane and rolled out from under him. He got to his feet, staggered, righted himself. He still had the gun and Zane hadn't the strength to get up and fight.

Muir saw the blood roiling across the rock—

"Zane!"

"Aw, ain't that sweet. Say your goodbyes, honey," Danny G said as Muir hurried forward, tears in her eyes. But instead of comforting Zane, Muir veered and bullrushed Danny G, hitting him squarely in the midsection and driving him backward. He managed to fire off a shot that clanged off the rock, kicking up shards and dust, but her force and technique, like that of an offensive lineman—or more exactly, rugby woman—sent him back and over the rimrock, screaming as he fell.

Muir struggled not to go with him, trying to reach for a handhold on the rock, but momentum carried her down —

A hand grabbed her ankle, halting her fall. Zane's.

Wounded or not, he was a strong man and legendary among his fellow rangers for a reason. He pulled her back up onto the ledge.

"Some rugby move. Impressive," he said to her. Breathing with difficulty.

She had tears in her eyes. "I told you to go back. Why don't you ever listen to me?"

"Didn't seem like a good time to start."

The helicopter roared over their heads, coming in for a landing. It was a precarious spot to land and the chopper had to maneuver.

They spotted the pilot: Blake Wilson. And his terrified passenger: the Senator.

Blake brought the craft down with one strut on the very cliff edge. He hopped out, came running. He hugged Muir like there was no tomorrow.

"Daddy," she said softly, warmly, then disengaged. "I'm all right. We've got to get him to a hospital."

Blake went over, inspected Zane's wound. "Always taking the bull by the horns, eh?"

"Yessir. This time the bull got me."

"Not so serious. Yet."

"I can manage," Zane says.

"The hell you can," Blake says. "You're going for a ride. Give me a hand, dear."

Together and with Zane's effort they managed to get him to a standing position and started walking him to the helicopter.

"How in the world did you ever get here?" Blake asked Zane.

"Long story."

"He is so foolish. You couldn't make a man more foolish," Muir said.

Before he could say anything she shocked him with a kiss planted squarely on his lips. She didn't leave off either. They both enjoyed it.

"Er, folks…" Blake said, nodding toward the helicopter.

The Senator had gotten out of the helicopter and regained some equanimity.

"Thank God. You're gonna be ok, boy. The US government's on your side. Where's the perp?"

Muir said, "Down there somewhere," indicating the ledge dropoff. While they helped Zane into the chopper, the Senator went over and took a look. Came back.

"He's alive. Hanging on by the skin of his teeth, and whatever else he's got that still works."

Blake Wilson said, "Tell him he just shot the one man who could save him. Going to have to come back for you, Senator. You ok with that?"

"Hell yes."

Blake handed him a canteen.

"Fresh North Rim spring water. Best in the State in my opinion."

"All I need is a little bourbon. Don't worry about me, I've made it through hell, otherwise known as Congressional committee meetings. Get that young man to a doctor."

Blake nodded and in a moment, with Zane and Muir aboard, he fired up the helicopter and they headed off toward Grand Canyon village on the South Rim.

The Senator watched them go, then headed over to the ledge. Down below he could see Danny G, bloodied but alive, and indeed hanging on to a perch that gave new meaning to the word precarious.

"Help me!" Danny G yelled.

"I'm a United States Senator. We give a lot of funds for search and rescue efforts so I can assure you the team will be on its way."

"I'm dying here!"

The Senator reflected a long moment.

"Well," he said, "it's a free country."

In his helicopter Blake said to Muir, through his earphones and hers: "Don't let him squirm around too much."

"I'm doing my best. He's not used to doing what I say."

Zane asked through gritted teeth, "Why are you crying? I'm the guy who took a bullet."

"Right. Figure it out, you dummy."

"You saved my life," he said, with some wonderment.

"Don't give yourself too much credit. I was thinking about saving myself. You really think he'd have let me go?"

"Damn. For a minute there I thought I was falling in love with you."

More tears came and it took her a minute to respond.

"Don't waste your energy. You've done enough falling for one day."

He smiled. She kept crying.

Blake noticed another helicopter over the canyon.

"If I didn't know better I'd say he's heading toward Panorama Point. Can't be Russ McGuiness."

# Would-Be's

Jimmy was piloting Pat and Richardson Stark. He received a message, shouted into his mike.

"Hartley Trail!"

Richardson nodded.

The helicopter banked, headed that way.

Buster and Jimbo had to slow down despite themselves when they cruised past the main Grand Canyon Village. Here there were more cars and more people and it would not do to call attention to them or their mission.

"Look like you're interested," Buster said.

"In what?" Jimbo asked.

"Jesus," Buster spat, shaking his head. "Look, put on those ghetto shades and lean back so nobody can take you for a moron."

"This moron can shoot. I'm gonna take down that sucker and after, maybe I'll take you down."

"In your dreams, if you got any."

"Gonna get one right now. Drive on and shut the hell up."

"Negative. You got to navigate the GPS to this frigging trail."

"Hey, what do we do if he don't make it up? Can't wait all night, can we?"

Buster thought a long moment.

"Ask him."

So Jimbo dialed his boss and patriotic leader, concluding with, "We can't wait up all night. Real dark out there, pumas and shit like that."

He listened as Marshal Hood responded.

"Uh-huh, uh-huh. Ok, gotcha. Thanks for the clarification, sir."

He switched off, then to Buster: "Bet you didn't think I knew 'clarification.'"

"Guess you do, congratulations. So what is his clarification?"

"We stay till hell freezes over if we have to."

As Jimmy's helicopter approached Panorama Point, he happily relayed a message to his passengers: "They've got Muir, safe and sound. That was them heading back to post."

Pat Stark burst into tears; "Oh thank God." Richardson Stark hugged her close, but still had the wherewithal to ask Jimmy, "And that bastard who took her hostage?"

"Hanging around down there."

He nodded toward Panorama Point, coming into view. As he arrived and hovered over: "That's the Senator down there."

"Well let's give him a ride back."

"Not so easy to land, sir."

"I'm counting on you, Jimmy. So is the Park Service. Going to be a hell of a feather in your cap."

"Yes sir."

Jimmy maneuvered his craft, searching for a landing zone, thought he saw it near the small strand of trees behind the point. He descended.

The Senator was no pilot, but he was afoot on the target terrain and he saw no picnic spot awaiting the aircraft. In retrospect, he thought, Blake Wilson had done a hell of a job bringing his chopper down safely and surely. Jimmy, he saw now, looked neither.

The Senator flapped his arms, trying to wave him off, but Jimmy had his eyes and hands full.

As the helicopter came down, it clipped a tree, landed with a harsh jar and almost crashed, literally bounced, spun around. Pat and Richardson Stark freaked as Jimmy battled to keep his helicopter from scooting across the flat rock he'd been aiming at and over the cliff.

It slid, slid—and came to a stop just at the cliff edge.

The Senator had been riveted, unable to approach too closely or do anything. Later he would say, "Weren't for those rotors I'd have grabbed that thing by the tail and hung on for their dear lives."

Now the rotors stopped. Seeing no movement, the Senator rushed forward, jerked open the door onto Pat. She looked shaken but whole. The Senator helped her out. She had trouble standing, so he lent her an arm.

"I'm all right," she said in a voice that trembled a little.

Richardson Stark came up to them, having climbed down from the other door. His head was bloodied but he nodded... he was ok.

Pat disengaged and said to Richardson, "Help him, Rich."

She meant the pilot. Stark went over and helped Jimmy climb out of his seat and onto terra firma.

He looked rattled and sounded like it but did his best to recover. In a weak voice: "Sorry for the inconvenience, sir. The downdrafts—"

"Forget it, boy, you got us here. What I want to know is, can you get us out."

This did indeed make Jimmy hesitate, before he rallied and mustered enough grit to say, "Whenever you say, sir."

"That's the boy," the Senator chimed in, "the kind of guts that made America great."

"Where is he? Has he been disarmed?"

"Mr. Stark, he needs both his arms right now, but if you mean firearms, see for yourself."

Stark headed toward the rock shelf at Panorama Point where Danny G had gone over. Richardson Stark followed, and despite her trepidations, Pat followed.

"If y'all got a rope in that chopper, we can bring the bastard up and make a citizen's arrest."

They all peered over the rim edge.

Danny G was not to be seen.

"He's escaped!" Richardson lamented.

"Don't think so, Mr. Stark," the Senator corrected. "That drop is sheer. He couldn't hold on any longer. Or else…he didn't want us to bring him to justice. Some perps are like that. Too gutless to take their punishment. No sir, he's gone to his Maker. And then he's gonna be sent on a one-way ticket to hell."


Buster and Jimbo reached the dirt road into the plateau forest leading to the Canyon Rim and Hartley Trail. As challenged as they were in terms of orientation and overall brain power, Marshal Hood had given them precise directions and they had GPS. In his time Hood had been an adventurer and lone wolf hiker who went off main trails and lived for back-country isolation. His detractors said he'd taken too much peyote and cactus juice and that plus many hours and days in the fierce Western sun had charred his judgement. Other said his judgement had been skewed at birth.

His followers said he had no need for divine judgement because his own proved divine—at least in their calibrations. The lonely, misbegotten, aggrieved, fanatic—Marshal Hood welcomed them and gave them a purpose.

Buster hardly slowed as he screeched off the highway and roared onto the dirt road, raising mounds of dust. Jimbo hung on, royally PO'ed at the assignment and Buster's driving, which threatened any minute to lead to a crash against some "frigging tree," he loudly groused.

"Wrap me around some frigging pine and I'll be coming for you," he scowled at Buster.

"Not if you're wrapped around a frigging pine tree," Buster came back, for good measure and because now he was PO'ed himself, making no effort to avoid the potholes that this back-backcountry road sported from erosion and complete lack of maintenance.

"You'll be picking cones out of your teeth."

Jimbo snarled, "Watch the fuckin' road."

Buster came back from the trees after taking a leak, zipping up his pants.

"Now I feel better. Coffee just goes right through me, you know."

"I didn't know and I could give a shit," Jimbo said ungraciously.

"You should. I'm your partner."

He took his rifle from where he'd propped it against the car's back fender, hefted it, admired it, began taking imaginary aim at a target. Which in this case, just discernible through the trees where they had parked off the ragged dirt road they'd navigated with great difficulty, was the trailhead for the Hartley Trail.

Buster continued,  "Got a good range from here. That sucker's gonna be huffing and puffing like it's his last breath, and guess what, it will be. Bet his head'll roll all the way back down to the river."

"Not today, boys."

B&J whirled and saw Sheri and Lincoln Williams training their service weapons right at them, specifically, Buster.

"Bet you didn't think us rangers could be armed and dangerous. Well this one is, and if you don't leave that rifle for the ants, I'm gonna get real dangerous."

"I don't believe you," Buster said.

Sheri fired off a shot that kicked up dust about a centimeter to the side of Buster's shoe.

"JESUS!" he yelled. Jimbo had jumped almost out of his seat.

"Way they do it in the Westerns, except next time you won't be able to dance," Sheri said.

Buster dropped his rifle on the ants' feeding ground.

"What's the charge?" Jimbo growled. "We ain't done nothing. You don't see me carrying."

"The hell you ain't," Buster barked at his erstwhile partner.

Lincoln smiled. "We'll find something. This is the Wild West, remember."

## The Dust Settles

When the dust had settled and helicopters made their way back to port, Blake Wilson was able to take stock of who, when and where.

The State Police had arrived and were writing out a report, aided by available witnesses.

The Senator was saying to his assistants, "I was impressed, impressed with the work of the National Park Rangers today. Write that down, Susie. When the reporters arrive, and they will, you'll have some quotes all ready."

The Senator turned to Blake Wilson.

"If I have anything to do with it, you're going to get that funding bill."

Blake smiled, nodded, answered before the Senator could ask.

"Zane Bailey's going to be fine. Muir said he's been giving her grief for one thing or another, and that's a good sign, and she's kind of looking forward to him going under anesthesia for a while."

He turned to Stark. "Richardson, why don't you have someone take a look at that bump. You too, Pat. I've seen a lot of delayed reactions to shock and stress."

"Like when we were married," she quipped, though this time he took it as a jest, and it was.

"More reason then to do what I said."

The pilot Jimmy had been hovering in the background, hoping not to be seen, much less heard. Blake turned to him: "After he's reamed you out, tell Russ to go easy on you."

"Yes sir," Jimmy said. "But you may see me tomorrow serving drinks or something at the Lodge."

When Lucinda Bailey closed the Backcountry Office, she hurried to the South Kaibab Trailhead to greet the mule train with the inner city kids.

They looked fit, some more than a little bit sunburned, and some tired, among them Lee.

Lucinda waited until Harvey finished a spiel involving condors, eagles and buzzards, and she gathered he'd waxed on somewhat about their various differences. He seemed to be even more than usually animated, discussing the birds' eating habits.

"Some might call them gruesome," he said to the group, "but nature's red in tooth and claw. That's a famous poem you kids should read, 'cause it says a lot about nature, and it's as true now as when it was written in the 19th century."

Lucinda asked Lee, "Tired from all this excitement?"

"Yes," he answered. "My head's about to blow up. Ranger Pine just stuffed it all up."

"Well, you might say you got a week's worth of campfire programs."

Lucinda announced, interrupting all talk and especially Harvey, "Muir Wilson's just fine, kids! Safe and secure and she got a helicopter ride to boot!"

They all huzzahed and cheered.

Harvey chimed in, "Courage and positive thinking, that's what you need in the wilds, kids. Not to mention a good helicopter."

He asked Lucinda sotto voce, "And the miscreant?"

"Buzzard food. But please don't tell them that, Harvey."

"Right, right," Harvey murmured, disappointed but understanding. Kind of.

# Recuperation

When Zane Bailey woke up from the operation to remove the bullet he'd taken, he had to admit he didn't expect to see the first person he saw at his bedside.

"How are you doing?" he managed to ask, fighting off the effect of anesthesia. "Kidnapping's traumatic. Get some counseling."

"Don't give me orders," Muir replied, "especially when you're thinking even less clearly than you usually do."

"Habit."

"Speaking of counsel, you've got some visitors. If you want my advice, you'll tell them to come back another day. You just got out of OR."

"Otherwise known as R&R. I feel fine."

"Actually I believe you. If anybody can take a bullet and keep on keeping on, it's you. They gave me the bullet in case you want it for a souvenir."

"Yeah. I'll use it for an earring."

"Geez, if I have to listen to this…"

She got up and moved toward the door.

"You been here all this time?" he asked. Surveying me?"

"Yeah, slow work day. Plus the trauma, you know, kidnapping. I'm not thinking straight."

He thought about saying, "Since when have you thought straight," but even though it might still remain true according to his principles, he felt despite the lingering anesthesia that this was neither the time nor place.

Plus he didn't want to say it. Strange.

She opened the door slightly, just enough to let in Blake Wilson. Zane couldn't quite make out from his perspective who the other prospective visitors might be, hanging in the background. He would converse with them in good time, he thought. Or bad time as the case would be.

Blake Wilson was always welcome.

"Not staying long, Zane," he said. "You may be an Iron Man but when the knife goes to work on you, you've got to let the stitches do their job."

"And my job?"

"You're on suspension, for going incommunicado when your boss needed to contact you. That's a major fault. I'll decide when the suspension ends, assuming you still want the job. At present I can tell you it'll be around the time the doctors give you a green light. So I can alert obnoxious tourists to trash their matches. But do us all a favor, eh. Take the time you need. That's your boss speaking."

"Thank you, sir. I'd say tomorrow or the day after—"

"The hell you will," Muir interjected.

Amazingly, that shut up Mr. Zane Bailey for a long moment. Blake smiled.

"She saved my life. I've got to listen," Zane finally said.

"And you saved hers, tit for tat, let's don't go over old ground." Blake said. "That's a father talking now, not your boss." He paused a moment, moved.

"I can never thank you enough. But I'll keep trying. Before, during and in between your future suspensions."

He turned and headed out, still moved and not trusting himself to get too sentimental and more teary-eyed than he already was.

He paused before going out.

"Sure you want me to open this door?"

"Something tells me it might be worse than a gut shot. But hell, bring 'em on."

Richardson Stark walked in, trailed by the Senator, his assistant and lastly, Pat Stark with a bouquet of roses.

"Every other day this young man becomes a hero. Twice in one week—I'd call that superhero," Stark said. He grabbed Zane's hand, pumped it vigorously. "Son, ask whatever you want. You've got a blank check, courtesy of yours truly."

"Easy, Richardson, he just got out of the OR," Pat cautioned.

Zane did his best to force a smile. "Thanks but, I wouldn't know what to buy with it. I'm a simple guy with simple needs."

The Senator, uncharacteristically not hogging the scene, bellowed.

"If I've got any influence on our great nation's lawmakers—and I like to think I do—you're going to be getting a medal, and not just any medal either. Something that glitters like gold, if you get the hint. Shoot, maybe two. We can do that, can't we Susie?"

"Whatever," she answered. "You're the boss."

"Glad you remembered that." To the others: "She forgets sometimes. Young."

"Maybe Mr. Bailey would like some rest," Muir said, annoyed at their obstreperousness.

Zane said, "Mr. Bailey appreciates those flowers, Mrs. Stark."

"Call me Pat," she said, finishing placing the elaborate bouquet on his bedside table. "Flowers do so lift one's spirits. I should know, thanks to you. Others could learn from your example."

"I copy that," Richardson smiled.

Zane said, "If you really want to help me heal in body and mine, cancel Paradise Estates. Or else turn it into a campground."

Richardson Stark reacted politely, "Well now I'll think about that on my way to the sites in question. Got a rendezvous I just can't miss. Have to leave the field to my family, Muir and Pat."

"Please do," Zane said to Stark's puzzlement, so he added, "leave the field."

"Right, right..." Stark said, though he wasn't agreeing, and this time not smiling, looked a tad uncomfortable. "Senator..." He shook hands with the honorable gentleman, hurried out with a wave to the others.

"Something I said?" Zane asked.

The next day some of Zane's colleagues visited in a group, Blake Wilson's idea, the better to ease the fatigue of recuperation. Zane forbore telling his chief that he didn't feel any fatigue at all, and in fact wanted very much to join in the search for Danny G's cadaver, which had proved unexpectedly difficult to locate.

"Maybe he fell into a big old hole," Lincoln Williams joked, "saving us the trouble of bringing him out."

"The Canyon doesn't need his kind of pollution," Zane countered.

Lucinda said, "I scrambled down here there and everywhere, but no sign. Could a puma have carried him off?"

"That's 100 per cent possible," Harvey Pine said. "Those big cats can do stuff you couldn't even imagine. Though I could.

"We'll keep looking. And thanks for the offer of help, Zane, but...no," Lincoln declared.

"I got me a merit badge, thanks to you," Lily smiled at Zane.

She'd been watching and waiting for most of the day and got the news about Zane and Muir late. "I saw some rafters but nothing else except some ravens and eagles and spirits of the Canyon, and I was about to sing a sunset song when I look and see this guy floating right down towards me, pack downwards and ready to turn into a hypothermia popsicle."

"So I got out that rope I'd brought for Muir and lassoed the boy before he went on down to Lake Mead. Just in time."

She'd hauled him onto the bank and managed to resuscitate and recharge his batteries. "It helped that his buddies came running over from where they'd encouraged this idiot, excuse me, unfortunate Canyon visitor, with lots of vodka. Had some left and it came in handy, because it would have taken too long to cut out some of the right cactus juice."

"I bet that cold water taught him a lesson," Harvey affirmed. "He got spread-eagled and then some."

Harvey continued, excitedly, "I went looking for that rattler, Zane. Didn't find him but I assure you I'm going to keep looking."

"Why would you do that, Harvey?" Zane asked, genuinely baffled. "He's already done his worst."

"Not so, Zane my boy. He's got some venom back and look, it's not normal to sit there on that trail like he owns it. Rattlers rattle, then they move on and give right of way, you know that. This one is a stain on the species and if I can just track him down, maybe we can get some answers."

"How are you going to do that?"

"Territory. I'm betting this old sucker's got habits and just hangs out looking for the next hiker to suck on. A rattler gone bad, you might say."

"Harvey," Zane said, "the Hartley Trail doesn't get much traffic, you know that. And anyway, we need you for the campfire programs."

Harvey thought long and thoroughly. Finally nodded, agreeing with Zane's estimation of his priorities.

"Right as rain as always, Zane. You know, the Senator still had time to catch my presentation last night, one of my best if I do say so. But you might say he skedaddled down to Flagstaff."

"Government business," Lincoln deadpanned.

"Yes," Harvey agreed, "named Susie."

They all stared at him, speechless, and Harvey added, "I've given a great lecture on the birds and bees, folks."

Raymond Gunther had stopped by on his way back from a long day welcoming visitors at the kiosk stand he'd maintained for so many years. "That old seat's got my butt imprints," he told Blake Wilson. "You might say I fit right in."

"So you did in mine. People say you gave orders and wore the chief badge like you'd been doing that for the last 40 years. Responsibility sat well on your shoulders. What do you say I recommend you for a post? Any place but mine. I've got a feeling you won't have to wait long for something to open up that suits you."

Raymond did give the possibility some thought—about 30 seconds worth—before saying, "My shoulders like lifting brochures, Blake. If I did become a boss man, sooner or later I'd run into a situation I wouldn't know how to handle. And it would eat at me now and forever. I've got me a niche and whatever comes my way, I know how to handle it. Call me an old fogey if you will."

"No, I call you an old pro. What's keeping you from your butt niche?"

Raymond smiled a yard or two wide and headed back to that small part of the world he knew and loved and where as he once said to Blake Wilson, "I'd like to be buried there, standing up."

## "Go Take a Hike" Becomes an Invite

Muir Wilson was deeply conflicted about Zane Bailey. She knew this even before he announced to her during one of her convalescent visits, "I am deeply conflicted about you."

He had accepted being suspended once again by the Head Ranger, Mr. Blake Wilson, for not following orders and going off "like the frigging Lone Ranger" in pursuit of Danny G without backup and even worse, communications updates.

"We didn't know where the hell you were," Blake thundered after he had put aside his copious expressions of gratitude for saving his daughter's life. Work did after all have certain exigencies.

Zane protested somewhat lamely, "I meant to call when I got satellite on the Hartley, but a snake interrupted me."

There too Muir was caught between chewing him out for confronting a snake and moreover, continuing when he'd been struck, albeit glancingly, and the courage and fortitude he'd shown which she had to admit, surpassed even her own. The swelling looked like it was subsiding—finally. So she indulged in a chewout session that lasted quite some time.

"You could have died," she said eventually, breaking down in tears, "playing fucking Don Quixote."

"What?"

"You wouldn't understand. It's called literature."

Tears, real and genuine and sincere. Ergo the conflict. She could not forget the sight of him rushing up the Hartley Trail, putting his life in jeopardy—and she was absolutely sure he didn't give a damn about his own life at that point if he could only save hers—and from afar, seeing the joy and relief on his face when he realized she was still alive and breathing on this earth.

But then again, he hated her job and everything having to do with it.

Which included her. "You're on the front line in the war against the environment," he declared, with a trace of regret, she thought. But just a trace. Hence, she supposed, his own conflict. By no means on earth—which she reminded him often, despite his skepticism, she loved deeply and dearly—was she going to tell him how many units she'd sold in just this week alone. She didn't need notches on her belt anyway, no matter how many more bonuses Richardson Stark ponied up for her.

"Nevetheless," he said during one of her after hours visits when his Ranger colleagues had left, the last being Harvey Pine who'd lingered long for a lesson on healing plants, and they were alone—she always took great care not to check her watch, for great fear he would bring down a voodoo curse on her "7 o'clock"—he said, rather solemnly as if this was a great, unprecedented moment: "I'd like to propose a hike."

She thought a moment. "You mean like, together."

"Took those darn words right out of my mouth."

"And you're darn happy about that, aren't you, because you'd have been obliged to say, 'with you.'"

"With you. See, I said it."

"Details?"

"Before my suspension ends."

"It ends the day your hospital stay ends. Really convenient, that. You can thank your boss."

"I'm bailing outta here early, like. I'm going bonkers hiking up and down these corridors."

"So are your nurses and care providers. All hours, each and every day. Frankly, I think they'll hold the door open for you. Whether you're on foot or crawling."

"On foot. With you. If you can get off from that miserable-earth-destroying job."

She knew she could, because business had been booming.

"I'll try. Business has been real slow."

White lie.

"Details?" she repeated. He outlined an itinerary. She said, "You'll still find blood on the rocks at Panorama Point. That's carrying masochism a little far, isn't it?" Adding, "You know, they still haven't found the body. He could still be hanging around there."

"Then we'll take a look as we pass by."

Pause.

"Together," he added.

She nodded. Ok.

# Hanging Around

Something about the Senator's sarcasm, allowing him the right to die, had given Danny G a shot of adrenalin. It reinforced tenfold his resentment of a US government that in his mind only served to oppress Godfearing, freedom-loving citizens like himself. Certainly he'd strayed off the straight and narrow path, but was that a path that patriotic spirits like him should take?

Certainly not.

For damn sure he wasn't going to go quietly into that good jail, and now, with juices pumping, he saw a way to slide across the cliff edge below Panorama Point where he'd found a lifeline handhold and reach ground flat enough for foot purchase. It would only take guts and a devil-may-care attitude toward the perdition that waited below if he slipped.

Five minutes later he reached ground and five minutes after that, again the Hartley Trail. He couldn't see the Senator above, which meant the honorable gentleman was idling away, waiting for rescue, without a thought to the citizen who just moments ago needed aid and succor.

His reward, Danny reflected, would be to get a shellacking prior to being tossed off the very promontory where that bitch Muir Wilson had caught him by surprise with a rugby slam. He was quite a bit shaken and had the bruises to show for it—those rock cliffs where he'd fallen and scrabbled were no picnic, and not least, his stomach hurt where Muir had rammed it with her shoulder. She'd have hell to pay for that, in the person of himself, Danny G Grissom.

It gave Danny G enormous satisfaction to think he'd be ridding Congress of a member who deserved to be replaced by a more like-minded Congressperson. No doubt Marshal Hood would be delighted to help fund their campaign.

When a second helicopter arrived, roaring into view, Danny G found luck on his side—he had tree cover at trailside. He hunkered down as the chopper rolled in, then heard the crash as it landed—as it were.

In seconds he made his choice—if he waited, help would arrive. It was basically now or never.

He hurried up the trail and topped out at Panorama Point. Luck stayed with him. He saw the Senator very occupied pulling out the shaken passengers.

Danny G had approximately 60 seconds to ascend the Hartley Trail to Panorama Point and round a curve that would block their view. In the background he heard voices—not the kind of tone that would signal alarm at spotting the fugitive. Rather, the "Are you okay?" variety.

He found this the stupidest question on earth. These people had crash landed and even if not dead, had had a hell of a shock. Goddamnit no, we are not okay.

But hell, he didn't care one way or another, except he hadn't been able to send the Senator to whatever land the honorable gentleman thought he'd been promised.

He was out of sight. Soon he would be out of their minds too, in the sense that they'd send out a search party in due time for his body which they'd assumed had joined the Grand Canyon geology.

But not today folks, no way. He had a trail to climb and in a few minutes, he was going to take a branch leading to a trailhead on the rim that hadn't been used for years, by anybody except former champion hiker and trailblazer Marshal Hood.

He still had Joe Blevins' phone, and there too, no one would be expecting a call from the grave. He had a feeling that Hood would be delighted to hear from an intrepid acolyte like him, who'd survived and shown he could out-tough and outfox those forces of oppression and suppression called law and order. But which he and Hood too called repression.

He by God had not been repressed, and he didn't plan to be any time in the future, which still lay ahead of him.

He was breathing hard, like a steam engine, but he was going to make it, and keep on making it. Making you might say, Trouble with a capital "T."

## PART 3

## On the Trail Again

Muir picked Zane up at the El Tovar parking lot.

She growled, "Please don't tell me you camped on the rim, one night after leaving the hospital. You don't think my father—excuse me—Ranger Superintendent Blake Wilson—would have given you a bed for the night?"

"Had to get some gear together."

"I do know you didn't spray graffiti on our property, because I just checked it out."

"All in good time."

"Look, consider this hike like the parole officer offering a cup of coffee to the parolee. Bonding it is not."

"As if I would want to bond with a capitalist stooge."

"Are we going to argue like this all the way to the North Rim?"

"Well, it's kind of like a habit."

"I'll give it a rest if you will."

He reflected.

"It's kind of like an addiction."

"Cold turkey. Yes or no."

He reflected again.

Asked, "Did you bring fresh or freeze-dried? Going to be a few long days, you know."

"Both."

"Good."

It was a long drive to the North Rim, circling around to the East, then heading north and west. They took Highway 89 and traversed plateau country, then angled west but rolled past the turnoff which led to the main, and only, North Rim village whose centerpiece, just recently opened for the season, was the Lodge, an historic structure not dissimilar to the magnificent El Tovar.

"Where we would go if you'd chosen a basic hike that normal people take," Muir remarked to her companion who'd just awakened from a cat nap.

"Normal and unadventurous."

"And completely remote. I'll be alone with you and a long way from rescue. If there could be a rescue."

"Let's don't break no legs," Zane said. "If you want to back out, call it before we go too far."

"I've already gone too far just getting here. I can't believe I'm doing this."

"You want to know a secret? Neither can I. Well?"

"Well what?"

"You going to back out?"

"You see a turn signal? Hey, what's in that duffel bag?"

"It stays in the car."

As he hadn't answered the question, she waited, casting glances that indicated she'd like a response. Finally:

"Stuff. Personal stuff."

"Keep your condoms to yourself."

"For myself, I don't need them."

She smiled.

"Touché. In more ways than one."

"Turn off there before this conversation gets more dirty than it already is."

She wheeled left onto a national forest road. They headed into the deep pinewoods, the trees looming very high above them and the cone-strewn land where they saw a deer from time to time and occasionally a squirrel. Pumas were here, no doubt taking a siesta after a long night of roaming and searching for prey. But one thing they did not see as they crisscrossed and turned from one road onto another, guided by

Zane who seemed to have memorized the labyrinthine route that would take them to the trailhead, was a human being.

They were a long way from anywhere, and Zane voiced his delight: "Into the forest primeval, solitude be praised."

"Like everyone says, you are one antisocial dude."

"Asocial. I can tolerate humans from time to time."

"Lucky me."

"Take a right."

They wound through the thick, immense forest on several more dirt roads that still had clumps of snow to remind them of a winter that had been, as usual, hard and long on the high North Rim.

"You're not using a map," Muir said to her companion.

"Hiked a lot in this forest. You can get lost real real easy, so I made it a point to GPS my brain."

"Ah, so that's why."

"I'm not going to ask you to explain that. I can tell you where we're heading, if you want to fill a corner of your brain."

"I'm guessing Dark Hollow."

"Bravo. Now I am impressed."

"My Dad took us on a lot of trips when he worked here. I got my first backpack when I was only six and we came here. Went down to Kanab Creek."

"A six-year-old on that trail," he said, even more impressed. "Hope you took a lot of candy with your gorp."

"I did and still do, and after you've finished making fun of me, don't expect any freebies."

"Hey, they're your teeth. Rot them if you will."

After what would seem to a first-timer a veritable labyrinth without end, a void loomed on their line of sight through the pines, a void called the Canyon. Muir pulled her 4x4 into a small clearing under the strewn cones of a giant pine. They'd come to the trailhead. It was just evident to their eyes when they scoped it out, a thin trail switchbacking down a slope that had no room for slippage.

"Well?" Zane said.

"Last one down doesn't get the girl," she said.

"I'll go first, okay?"

She smiled.

In a few minutes they'd verified their packs, particularly water gourds. Zane lifted out a gallon jug of extra water.

"When you're going to dry camp..." he explained. "I checked the weather a hundred times. You've got time to do that in hospital. The rainstorm that came through a couple of days ago probably left water in the potholes but you can never be sure."

Muir pulled back a tarp that had been covering her gear, and lifted out her own gallon jug.

"I learned that when I was six."

Before Muir locked the car and stashed her keys in her pack, she asked:

"What's in that duffel?"

"Some duct tape. Provisions."

"Provisions?"

"Extra. You know, like candy."


They stood a moment on the rim before descending to admire the view. It was different from that of the South Rim, Muir had always thought.

Darker, with more tree and verdure on the slopes—and if anything, more spectacular. The whole panorama, lit up by the still early morning sun, seemed to her to have fewer colors, but those it did seemed deep and dark, almost pristine and even prehistoric. Wild. Like the guy I'm with, she thought.

"I still can't believe I'm doing this," she said to him.

"You've done this area before," he said, "like you've been telling me over and over."

"Not with you."

"Ah, right."

"So from here, it looks too narrow. When I was six, I had some butterflies going down. But there's traction. More or less. I'll go first, so if I fall, you'll know where not to step."

"Yeah. And you know me well. I wouldn't want to interrupt my hike just because you plunged into oblivion."

"We're not down yet, mister cocksure. Let's see if you make it. What an idiot, taking a grueling hike with a bullet wound still in his gut."

"Hiking works out the kinks. That's just another one."

She stepped down onto the trail, and he followed.

On the ride over Zane had described the trail to Muir succinctly: "If you start to ascend, you've taken a wrong turn."

And so it was. The trail zigzagged in continuous switchbacks down a relentless descent. Far below, roughly a thousand or so meters, they could spot the Esplanade, the wide flat plateau which would be their first destination. At times the width of the trail contracted so much that they had to rush in long strides to a wider patch which, thankfully, lay just beyond the eroded section.

"Not for our friends suffering from vertigo," Muir remarked wryly.

"I don't have any friends," Zane said, "and if I did, I wouldn't take them down this trail."

"I believe you on both counts, and hey, take your foot out of your mouth, you'll need that foot."

Enough of the trail remained however for them to retain firm footing, and the hike down through rock and cliff and the frequent bordering pines and scrub revealed one magnificent vista after another.

They feasted on the views.

"Let's forget the chitchat," he said, "might cause us to miss the sights."

"Like I really have gossip to share with you."

Happily, neither suffered from each other's conversation and they reached the Esplanade soon enough despite their moderate pace and having to squeeze down a narrow rock chimney that gave onto a rock and shale scramble that lasted far longer than either would have liked.

Muir had always enjoyed the Esplanade, its flatrock making for easy hiking and all the more opportunities to revel in the great Canyon.

"Ready for adventure?" he asked.

"If I wasn't, I wouldn't have agreed to come along. A crazy wild man like you has the one feature that redeems him in my book—he can take you to places no one has seen before—or would want to."

"And that excites you?"

She started to say, "Yes because selling houses with the same spiel every day week after week can get godawful boring," but thought that would not only give him satisfaction, he would launch into a tirade that might distract him from routefinding—and not to mention, piss her off for the rest of their hike. And they'd made a kind of truce, after all.

So she just said: "Yes."

They headed west. One could have called it route finding but there was no route that she could discern. They were finding their way across the Esplanade, which was not difficult hiking, and both the views and landscape were beautiful, wild mixes of cactus and cactus flowers with the occasional blessed cottonwood tree which had found a home in a sandy bottom that was dry most of the year—and was now.

"Not a good sign," she said. "No pothole, no seep."

"We haven't finished our gallon yet," he offered. "And two litres in reserve. Unless you didn't pack what you were supposed to pack."

"Plus an orange. Citrus to wet the whistle at tea time."

They reached a lovely spot of slickrock and, indeed, a small spring that drip dripped, one by one. It would take an hour to fill a canteen, but time was getting on and...

"You want my opinion?" Zane asked.

"Never."

"This is a beautiful campsite. We could do a lot worse than Dark Hollow. And it's got water. Even if it's a drop at a time."

"Kind of like evolution. I can get behind the choice."

They set up camp and spent some time watching the sun light up rock and cliff as it angled downward toward the evening, each light beam different in brightness and shine depending on which spot "was lucky to receive the gold," she said matter of factly but he thought "verged on poetry."

They enjoyed the show, and she was surprised to find that he'd packed her favorite tea. He brewed her a cup. He qualified, "A little late for tea time but—"

"How did you know I liked this one?"

"Your mother. She spills secrets after a couple of glasses of wine."

"That's BS. You can do no wrong after that cactus flower. Which I have to say resembles those."

A cactus plant had taken root in a small garden underneath the cliff against which they had posed their packs, and against which they now leaned their backs, watching the sunset show.

"Picked it here, that morning," he said.

She thought a moment. "You're telling me you hiked to the river, floated across it on some kind of inflatable, then hiked up and out and knocked on our door with a cactus rose in hand?"

"The very same. Sorry I was late. You were right to be upset. We got off on the wrong foot so to speak. I should have brought one for you."

"And drowned. Somehow I get this image of you holding it in your teeth while you crossed the river. And two would have capsized the boat. Right?"

He didn't answer directly, just held out his hand.

"Is the second time a charm?"

This rose beamed in the waning light. She took it and tried to think of something to say that would not sound too bestruck, but still appreciative of his romantic gesture.

As for Zane, he couldn't believe his luck in finding the bloom. Most of the other cacti they'd come across had shed their flowers a week ago, as the plants only sprung to brilliant florescence once a year. One had to seize the moment. He waited, wondering, but he thought he saw her softening. That in itself was enough for him.

"I didn't think there was a sweet bone in your body. I was wrong," she said.

She breathed in the scent, closed her eyes, enjoying it.

"They say it can be worn in your hair," he said.

"Do they? I'll consider it."

"It occurs to me I've never seen you with your hair down."

"Well, that will be one special day for you, yes?"

"Yes."

"Who's cooking tonight?"

He was. He prepared a dinner with fresh food that had managed the first day's trail. Thereafter, he knew, they would have to go cans and freeze-dried.

"Packed this too," he said. "Best to drink it now, Less weight to carry."

It was, of course, a bottle of wine.

"Sorry," he said, "my credit card couldn't match Richardson Stark's and this one's not so high class."

"Neither is Richardson. And you don't have a credit card. It'll do."

His little camp stove did its job, reliable as always, and she helped with the camp plates and cups and poured the wine while he served.

Both, they found, had learned the camper's trick of propping up and reclining comfortably against their backpacks while they ate.

"It's called a BACK pack after all," she said.

Afterward they sipped wine and watched the night sky festooned with stars.

"I grew up in Los Angeles," Zane said. "Won't even tell you which suburb—what difference would it make? They sprawl and sprawl. Once thousands of orange trees blossomed in the basin. Then the people came. Now you are one very lucky dude if you have a garden with an orange tree.

"My family, such as it was, didn't. Most days when I got old enough, which was pretty damn young, frankly, I hitched to the beach. Had a goal in between waves to count the sand grains. Got pretty far but needless to say, a lot got left to be done."

Muir was amazed to hear him open up. She laid it to the wine, which as he said did not match her stepfather's El Tovar choice in pedigree or price, but went down very well.

"Every wine tastes better out here," he said, reading her thoughts.

His own thought was, "Even you," but he didn't dare say it. She was tolerating him and his company, and that was a giant step.

It did not take long for the night sky to burst with a thousand lights. They took turns identifying the constellations, and both were surprised to find that they each could, with great accuracy.

She said, "It may also surprise you to know that I love this planet to the bottom of my heart, as pretentious as it sounds. We send satellites around the solar system, we've got giant telescopes now in space that can see almost to the beginning of the universe, we look and look—and we haven't yet found a planet that looks as beautiful and amazing as ours. Rivers, streams, canyons, mountains. And species. So many, so different, all of them. People should wrap their heads around that incredible fact every single day."

"Or hour. You're preaching to the converted."

After a moment, he said:

"Didn't expect that from you. Honestly."

"Like you really knew me in any way, shape or fashion."

"Right."

"But you know, you can't punch out people who don't get it."

"Why not?"

"There's too many of them."

"Why I take refuge in places like this. I won't make a good husband. Home and hearth and all that."

"I haven't proposed." He laughed, which she again laid to the wine's effects. She liked the sound and the way he looked when he laughed. No doubt it was the wine also acting on her.

As for Zane, he kept watching the stars and tried not to look at her. As much as he respected women's rights, or thought he did, he feared that out here, under the heavens, he would view her through the prism of romance and, it had to be confessed, sex. Even perhaps, love. He hadn't expected to be so susceptible.

He did now however sneak a look. It confirmed his susceptibility.

At that very moment she said, "Look!"

She pointed toward the cliff edge in the distance where, suddenly, a beacon of light had appeared. Like moonlight, it spread slowly into the canyon hollow where they had camped. Its origin:

"My God, that's Jupiter," he marveled.

"Since when does a distant planet like that shine like moonlight?"

"Since I guess it approached closer to the Earth. They say it hasn't happened in 70 years."

He stared. The light from the planet cast rays of light less broad than the moon's when full, or even half-full, but resplendent in the Grand Canyon night.

"We are very lucky," she said softly.

"Really," he agreed. "They say Jupiter is the planet of luck and good fortune. Let's cross our fingers and enjoy it. Who knows where we'll be in 70 years. The Canyon will be here, fates and geology willing. But us..."

"I've never called you by your first name."

The non-sequitur came so unexpectedly that he turned again to look at her, puzzled.

She had taken her hair down.

"Zane," she said.

That was that. He couldn't help himself, but before he could lean in to kiss her, she did it to him.

Muir had made a decision, though she well knew it wasn't completely rational. Feelings never were. Call it the wine, or the Canyon, she thought in the heat of a very heated moment, followed by him laying their camp mattresses side by side.

They made love, and she found it more exciting than with her previous lovers. They weren't numerous, and she'd thought that it was just a matter of time, or numbers, for her to find more satisfaction. And here, now, time and numbers coalesced.

She held him close, hugged him tightly. She caressed the muscles in his back, hard and wound tight as steel cords almost—fruit of a hundred hikes in magnificent places on the Earth like this one.

He found her caresses, scratches almost, utterly exciting, and made love to her again. Muir had never given herself to a man as she did now, coming in waves of ecstasy she thought only existed in cheap romance novels. But no. Here she was, and here it happened.

They lay long moments in silence, tranquil. One could say, genuinely happy. Finally she said, looking up at the giant planet and its long rays illuminating their canyon and cliffs, genuinely astonished she could say something like this: "Thank you, Jupiter."

"Thank you. Muir."

The next day they continued down the hollow, passing some wonderful small copses of cottonwoods and a small waterfall that poured over flat shale rock. She proposed a pool bath to "clean the dust that's been formed by millennia," but he countered, "If it's that ancient it should be registered as an historic archaeological monument. Leave it, government orders."

"Ok, next one."

"I've got a place in mind if you're willing to drop the pretentiousness."

"Agreed. Just this once."

And a half hour later they came to a veritable pool in the desert, wider than a bathtub, smaller than a pond. In short, just right for a desert cooler.

"Last one in's a drunken Ranger," she quipped.

"That would be me. In my stupor I imagined you slept beside me. Or more accurately, with."

"Keep dreaming, it's healthy exercise."

They basked in the natural springwater pool together. It was icy cold but they had had the luck to arrive at the moment when the sun was direct and the heat just ideal "to warm body and soul," Muir said.

"There's another way," he said.

"Don't you have anything else on your mind?"

"Not this particular moment."

"Well, if it will help get your mind on more constructive pursuits…"


In the afternoon they explored the wonderful canyon with frequent detours to small side canyons. They were moving down deeper and deeper and the cliff walls rose higher and higher. The sunlight arrived directly only an hour or two each day, and they hiked in shade while far above the sun "blessed the land," Zane ventured.

"I thought you were not religious."

"Only here."

That evening they made camp at a spot he knew and liked, and she seconded, at bankside where the canyon stream was dry, and smooth shale shelves extended along the streambed as well as banks, so they had smooth surfaces for their camp mattresses.

"For the sake of appearances," Muir said, "I'm claiming this spot"—in the hollow underneath an overhang created by the smooth rock.

"Who's going to alert the newspapers and mags? I don't see anybody here, there or anywhere."

"Hawks and eagles. Don't underestimate their salacious curiosity."

"Well, I know they're salacious. Whether they're interested in us…"

Later that night, this time waiting and watching for the arrival of Jupiter—it did not disappoint—she came back to his side.

He said, "That's what I like being here, with you. Nobody is around to be interested in us but us."

"It'll be different back home. So to speak."

"Don't rain on our parade."

She snuggled close. If perchance it did rain, she thought, he would do for a poncho, and the rock shelf behind her for a shelter. For the moment, here, she thought, she had no need whatsoever for back home. Here she had everything she needed, and in the person of the man holding her close with a tenderness she would have never believed possible from him, more.

Zane Bailey did not believe in heaven, or that it could be better than this, in his beloved Canyon, with her.

They spent the next few days moving deeper into the canyons leading to the largest system carved by Kanab Creek.

They boulder-hopped, contoured around others, waded through pools that lingered and refilled canteens at Shower Bath Spring, enjoying the green fern oasis formed by the lifegiving water.

Each campsite brought solitude and wonder, and prepared them in stillness and repose for the trial that would come on the grueling talus that would have to be traversed at the Colorado. The river itself seemed as full and strong as ever, but Zane demurred. "It's gone down," he said. "Either a decision at the dams upstream or just plain drought. More of the same. In a few years we'll be thirsty. Very thirsty."

She said, extremely tentatively and after all kinds of hesitations, because she knew he detested Lake Powell, or more properly, what had formed it: "The dam has saved us for a little while."

"From our own folly. It flooded the most wonderful canyons on the river and gave people the impression they were living in Babylon. Southern California used to be livable, or barely. I should know. But people kept coming. Breeding and demanding water for their swimming pools. You've seen Vegas and Palm Springs. Oases become abominations."

She regretted bringing up the subject.

"Cloud just covered the sun. Let's hit the talus."

For the next few hours they clambered. Up, over and around the boulder field that stretched for over five miles at riverside, always unable to get a consistent rhythm in the jumble of rocks that had slid down from above and now blocked verdure and beaches being formed.

It was terrifically hard, hot work, with no respite because they wanted to get to their campsite above Deer Creek Falls before noon. The sun broiled even this early in the morning, but enough clouds scudded across to give them interludes of shade. They were in great shape before the hike and even more now, but still they welcomed the breaks from the brutal sun. "We're kind of lucky," she said, meaning the clouds, trying to not let him notice the halt in her respiration.

"I've never had luck," he said, "must be all you."

"Once. Once you had good luck," she said, topping a boulder and noticing a rattler in the blistering rocks at waterside. Enough paces away so that she didn't pause a second but definitely picked up her pace insofar as possible.

"In not stepping on that little guy? I saw him a mile way. Or almost. He's not lying low."

"It's his territory. We're just visiting."

"This particular territory he can have."

"Agreed."

"First time you've done that."

They went on another mile or so, then another, hiking and working hard.

"Almost home," Zane said, nodding toward the patch of wet sand up ahead where Deer Creek formed a towering cascade. It was plunging at full force, replenished by the spring rains, and its roar resounded in the otherwise silent canyon.

"What good luck were you talking about?"

"You've been racking your brain for the last hour about that?"

"Yeah, and it's damn well racked."

She gave him a moment of suspense before answering, and as he seemed finally about to scream with frustration, answered: "I agreed to come with."

At Deer Creek Falls civilization in the form of a party of rafters jarred them temporarily out of their idyll. But their reentry went more smoothly because Zane had timed their arrival to synchronize with Dock Curry's stopover.

While his latest party of sunburned tourist/adventurers gamboled about taking photos and marveling at the lovely falls that pounded the small sand beach below before joining the mighty river, the hikers shared memories of Dock's previous trip.

"I'd like to thank you so much," Muir said, "for how you dealt with the kids. One of them even told me he wanted to be a river guide like you when he grew up."

"Hell," Dock said, "I need him now. Give him my number and tell him to grow up fast. Maybe he won't bail out on me like you did."

"She's stuck with me so far," Zane smiled. "Charity I guess."

"Could be both decisions were a mistake," she countered.

They waited till the rafters relaunched, waving and watching them go until out of sight.

They hiked up the trail paralleling the Falls, alongside the stream that joined the Colorado below, creating lovely whorls of smooth rock and occasional plunge pools. Muir stopped for a moment to admire a cactus that had by choice or happenstance found a home near the bend where the trail topped out and the ascent gave way to a more gradual narrow winding route, quite precipitous, to the campground on a small plateau.

"Congratulations, little guy," she said, addressing the cactus, "you've found a good home with just enough water to live on, ecological, with a great view to live for." Zane was admiring it. They had lost sight of the Falls, but in the distance below they could see the Colorado, blue and beautiful in the midday sun. He added, "And smart too, 'cause he's taking water that would otherwise end up in somebody's swimming pool in LA."

"Agreed, but if he's that smart, he's a she."

Zane whirled. "I've converted you! Ecology over swimming pools."

"Not yet. But recently I acquired a new appreciation of cactus."


They spent an hour at one of the plunge pools. The water was cold but just bearable, and wonderfully refreshing in the heat and after the talus and more dust and sand.

"Do we have to leave?" Muir asked.

"No."

"Then let's don't."

But paradox of the desert—one could stay in the coolness of Deer Creek stream only so long. Hypothermia could be staved off for long, but no longer.

They hefted their packs and headed past the campground and toward a trail that climbed up and over a steep slope, a slog in the heat of midday. But they wanted to reach Surprise Valley and then descend to Thunder River.

They lunched there, lolled some time afterward in the shadow of the shortest river anywhere, bursting out of a sheer cliff and plunging a short way to the creek below and great river waiting for it downstream.

"For thirsty Los Angelenos," Zane remarked.

"Yes, but I'm going to fill up my water jugs and deprive them. It's a long way back to the Rim and I don't think we'll make it back today."

"We could. But the Esplanade awaits. And it's beautiful up there."

"Better fill up your jug, pardner."

They had left their packs at the Surprise Valley trail junction. Both lugged them and a gallon jug of fresh Thunder River water to the Wall, up a grueling series of switchbacks that seemed to go on and on.

But at sunset they arrived at the Esplanade. The slickrock here was warm and welcoming, and they laid out mattresses on the edge of the plateau.

"And if we get carried away?" Muir asked archly.

"Us? No way. But still, what a way to go."

"I promise to be kind and gentle tonight."

"That will be like a first, no?"

"Only where you're concerned."

They had reached a point during their wilderness escapade where they could muffle disagreements and different philosophies in jibes that were indeed kinder and more gentle—"at least by comparison," she qualified.

But that evening, after dinner and what might be, both thought to themselves, the last time they would ever be together like this, making love like this, on a night that promised to be windy, they reveled in the spring weather that sometimes augured new life and new worlds.

Both doubted they'd found either, but it was exquisite to lie together on the Esplanade, enjoying the breezes that swept across the Canyon, whirled around rock and river and reached them on their journey. They were just right, neither too strong nor too weak nor too intermittent. They lay there mostly silent, in the present, and much time passed before they slept.

After they'd reached the trail they'd descended days ago and busted guts on the ascent, they loaded up Muir's car and headed back.

They saw no other cars or tracks and realized once again how "lucky we've been," Zane said. "Pockets of wilderness and solitude to build the soul. Long may they remain. Pristine. Undeveloped."

The last word reminded her of their war, and she let it go. She knew that disagreements, pain and anger at such would come soon enough.

But they came sooner than she thought.

"Let me out here," Zane said.

They had reached the highway and she was about to turn east for the long drive back to the South Rim.

He got out, went to the back and pulled out his backpack and the mysterious duffle of other equipment—of one kind or other, she imagined.

She decided not to ask or speculate in his presence as to what the hell he had in mind.

"I don't like this. Whatever it is."

"That's why I'm not telling you whatever it is."

"When will we see you again?"

"Could be a few days."

"What should I tell your boss?"

"That I'm going solo for a while."

"For a while there I thought you'd become sensible. Whatever you're doing, I mean."

"If I'm lucky, I'll be back before the cactus blooms fade."

"Get lucky," she said softly.

He reached in and kissed her. She kissed him back, but not with the full fervor of the past few days. She knew he was going to do something she wouldn't approve of. Something she would consider foolish.

As per usual.

She drove off. He watched her go until she passed out of sight. Then he strapped on his pack and lifted the duffel, turned and headed down the highway, marching on plain road. It was one of the least traveled in America, but he knew his destination and it lay on it.

They didn't call him "Insane Zane" for nothing.

# A New Recruit

Marshall Hood looked reflective, which for an action man like him came as rarely as compromise. He had his beliefs and they moulded his values and he viewed them as iron hard, incapable of bending without ultraviolence to the laws of physics—about the only laws he recognized as not subject to his individual choice as to whether to obey them—but the man standing in front of him perhaps obliged a decision reset. Being an action man—he had pioneered so many back-country routes in his day, guiding the (literally) unwashed— he liked to make decisions quickly.

"I'm not a man who gets surprised. Can't afford it, don't want it, make sure if it happens, I tamp that sucker so far down it farts out with my supper. But you surprised me. And would you believe, I'm appreciating it. They left you for dead and you came back. Now what I want to know is, now you've become a ghost, what can you do for me?  Get him one of those peanut butter sandwiches, Buster. And take one for yourself. You got to chow down before you start on that slammer food."

Buster took the flak and docilely fetched the sandwiches from a tray next to the enormous outdoor barbecue grill where Hood was sitting with his interlocutor, Danny G. The escapee was bruised and scratched but otherwise sipped a Budweiser with his usual ease.

He eyed Buster and smirked.

"Sent out a boy to do a big man's job. Get what you pay for."

"That I did. That I did. But I'm thinking I've got a replacement who's shown me some serious survival capabilities.

Someone who'll let bygones be bygones, just like I did when I agreed to send Simone to fetch you."

"Now that was a plus, I got to say."

"She's no roll in the hay and only, if that's what you're thinking. She's got skills. Just like that lady who sent you ass-downwards."

Danny G crushed his empty beer can with more force than usual, enough to cut his palm and bring blood.

"Gonna take her out, with or without your permission."

"Now I can't say I approve of that radical revenge notion. On the other hand, I didn't appreciate getting hoorahed in the presence of a United States Senator. If Mr. Wiseass Blake Wilson loses his one and only daughter, I can't say I'd feel his pain."

"On it."

"Not yet you ain't. Take some days here at our facilities to rest and relax and get your mojo 100% back. Then maybe we'll furnish the equipment you need. You do that, you'll be my new favorite son. In the meantime, I don't know your real identity, Mr. Zach Taylor. So if somehow you fall back into the hands of our state's so-called law and order, well that'll be another one of those unwelcome surprises I hate so much."

"Won't take me long to recuperate. I got a lot of adrenalin in stock."

"Buster's busy with his peanut butter. See old James Monroe over there. He'll show you around."

"He don't look near as good as Simone."

"She's candy all right. But first you got to know where to find her." He yelled over to the hulk that he called Monroe, "Give him the full tour, James." Turning back to Danny G: "Tomorrow I'll lecture you on the virtues of discipline we teach here. And our missions. I'll be expecting your full concentration. Good to remember that."

"When I got to, I remember everything. Some people are gonna find that out. Subject to your timetable, sir."

Hood smiled, a genuine smile. "That's the talk I like to hear."


It didn't take long for Danny G to adjust to Hood's Western Marshals, as a great deal of time was devoted to military-style training and gaming special ops. He liked both, and he was surprised to find there was no lack of ammo on the premises.

"Surplus stores," Hood told him after a couple of long days where he laid low and essentially "bored the hell out of myself."

"Time to move to the next stage of your membership," Marshall Hood said. "Preparing mind and body for missions where you kick butt and take no prisoners. That's a crude way to describe what we do and what we're going to do."

"I take that literally," Danny G said, "and let me say, until I was interrupted and bad luck intervened, I had no intention of keeping my recent prisoner in good health."

"We've got a world class firing range here. Show me what you can do."

Danny G proved up to the challenge. In the past he'd worked on his skills for many hours and days, with ammo he could beg borrow or steal, mostly the latter, and even his rap songs took a distant second place to more or less blowing the hell out of whatever target he aimed at.

Rumor had it that during his course of lawbreaking activities he'd put said skills to use in a real world environment.

Danny G never confirmed that—he wasn't born yesterday—but he liked to say, "I've gone through three belts before this one. Only so many holes you can put in 'em, if you know what I mean."

In front of his nominal boss, he took real glee in blowing holes in bullseyes that "were too dumb to haul ass out of the way."

"Well and good," Hood said, "but can you hit moving targets? The ones that do haul ass?"

"Let's just say, I've had some practice."

Hood reflected a long moment.

"You're ready," he said.

## Insane Zane

Zane Bailey had only hiked a few miles along the big wide and lonely highway leading eventually to St. George, Utah, when a refitted 4x4 that looked as if it dared anyone to cut in front—because from the looks of it, this vehicle had road rage written all over it—slowed beside him.

Zane had no intention of hitchhiking, but the driver jumped to conclusions. He pulled over on the shoulder and waited for Zane.

"Heading somewhere in particular?" he asked.

"Yeah. West."

"On foot? You're gonna be all chewed up by the buzzards before you get anywhere except the place I'm going. Hop in."

Zane hesitated.

"Your ass is gonna be real lonely before the next car comes along. That ole sun's going down and so's traffic."

"Appreciate the offer," Zane said, and opened the passenger door.

"You ask me, you're heading for Hood's Western Marshals. Looking like an eco-freak, now that's good, bait and switch you know. Except we don't care, you know. You know how to put a Javelin anti-tank buster on your shoulder and fire it, no questions asked, I guarantee you. Thing is, you look like a tree hugger, he's gonna ask you some questions. You got answers?"

"Yeah? Right here."

Zane pointed to the big Bowie knife strapped around his waist in a leather scabbard. Muir had seen and admired it and it had come in handy for some camp cooking chores.

The driver whistled.

"My name's George. George Washington. On account of I was the first recruit. Yours?"

"Grover Cleveland."

George chuckled. "You ain't been accepted yet and you're thinking right already. A hard rain's coming down, Grover, just a few days away. You want to be part of it, work on your firearm skills. We got some trainers'll whip you into fighting shape right quick."

"I got a friend just joined. Sent me a text and said it was the place for me. I don't have many friends, you know. Lot of people are scared of me. Danny's his name."

"We don't got anybody named Danny."

Zane hid his disappointment.

George said, "We don't use real names. If you got any brains besides that big mother knife, you'd have figured it out. Only the Boss knows our real names, and most of 'em he's forgot. A name's a name. A firearm, why that's what made America the great country it is. Or was. We're gonna make America great again."

"Catchy. Should be a slogan."

This merited a long look from George.

"You been living under a rock or something?"

"Kind of."

"Well slide out and smell the flowers."

They rode in silence for a while because George was thinking hard.

"Your friend, he brown-haired and kind of tall, looks like some bar fights put his face through a meat grinder?"

"Yeah, most of the bars won."

"Could be Zach. He stays out of sight. Like it's his preference. Or else Simone. She keeps a man busy till she gets bored and drops him like a stinky turd. I got a month's worth, and that's a record if you ask me. Looks like you might have a happy reunion."

"Yeah, except everything I just told you is bullshit. I'm here to hike, and I need transport to the trailhead."

He put the knife to George's throat.

"Pull over, you moron fascist."

George did, forthwith.

"Another second of your horseshit and I'd have cut your throat for real. You're walking. Don't forget to smell the roses on your way."

"That's ten miles! And it's gettin' dark."

"Got a good moon tonight. Not that you deserve it. Follow it or your nose."

"That's a company car!"

"Pick it up on the way. Now get lost, literally."

He sped away. George saluted his departure with a thunderstorm of curses and generally words no decent mother would ever condone. But the 4x4 was gone.

George did come upon the vehicle again about two miles from the Hood compound. His relief gave way to more anger though when he looked inside and found the keys missing. He looked all over the truck, the road, and then into the forest until the darkness deepened and temps plummeted. He hadn't worn his heaviest coat and knew he'd better haul ass back to all the like-minded patriots who he knew would be waiting for him, and would be as pissed as he was when he got back and recounted his ordeal.

Unfortunately, he found Marshall Hood was more pissed at him.

"You let some candy ass longhair—"

"Shorthair—"

"That's a metaphor, dumb ass! For some pussy nematode-lover who handed your ass to you! I don't give a damn he had a big knife. Where was your big knife?"

"Sir, you know, he's still out there in the woods and I—"

"Congratulations. You're got an ounce or so of brains. Tell Jimbo and Zach to get their firearms. And I don't mean their cap pistols."

"The new guy?" George objected. "Could be this freak is his friend. He was asking about new recruits."

Hood paused in his reaming.

"You know what that tells me? FBI."


"I concur in that estimate," Danny G said. "Ain't any of my friends walking around without cuffs."

"I'm glad you concur, because you're gonna go along with Jimbo and George here. That is, if you're not too pussy-whipped."

Danny G realized that much as Marshall Hood preached individual freedom and don't tread on me, he had sources of info that probably ranged from hidden video to roaming ears. Thus he knew he'd just crawled out of the hay with Simone, and been none too delighted about leaving it. Simone, he thought, could do a number on any redblooded man.

"I'm gonna skin him alive. Unless of course you want him breathing."

"From what I've said you don't get the picture? I'm real disappointed in you, Zach."

The man he called Zach looked stern, all business—his kind of business.

"Copy that." He turned to Jimbo and George. "Stay out of my way."

They took a jeep to the abandoned 4x4. Got out and armed themselves with all the hardware at their disposal.

"Shouldn't we look for the keys?" Jimbo asked.

"Go right ahead," DG said. "I'm going huntin'."

"Hard to track him. All those pine needles don't leave much of a trace."

"I got a nose and a pair of eyes. Enough for me, boys. Watch out for flak."

He moved into the woods.

After a moment, Jimbo turned to George and indicated an area of forest to check out, then pointed to the area where he wanted to go.

Neither was on the same side of the road as Danny G. The zealous recruit liked it that way, thinking that even if the tree-kissing bastard was munching gorp in their neck of the woods, Jimbo and George wouldn't know which end of a gun to aim. Hell, they probably thought "stand down" was the opposite of stand up.

He, Danny G, had no intention whatsoever to yell stand down or anything else, and for damn sure, not ask any questions. His bullets were going to eliminate any need for that. He intended to scout this area, then move over to the other. And if the nature boy, whoever he was, had moved deeper into the wilderness, he'd be back and like the Terminator, finish his business. Danny liked the gig he'd found, and he especially liked his nights with Simone, the alley cat who knew guns even better than she knew how to have fun, and that was considerable. Danny G knew, because he had a hell of a lot of experience with brief stands in the sack, that she'd move on one day, or night. But not soon, and a hell of a lot later than with some of the rube trash Marshall Hood had been collecting.

He walked nonchalantly, scanning the woods that here nearer the North Rim were thick and deep. Lots of space between the big trees however, and ergo less room for the game he was hunting to take cover. Sooner or later, and sooner he thought, he'd catch sight of his quarry, who'd probably expected some sort of reprisal, sometime, on the part of Hood's Western Marshals, but not the shooting kind.

Danny G was going to take him down, and one shot ought to do it. He would call the rubes to come over and inspect his kill, and they would be so impressed they'd lug the body to a disposal site forthwith, no objections.

The pine needles swished and hissed as he passed, but given the terrain, and the very same needles, he had no fear of being ambushed. And he was sure as sure could be that the fugitive, as he considered him, had no firearm. Against the eco-freak code.

Danny G walked for most of an hour, not in a direct line, but rather circling and branching, covering as much terrain as possible. He was disappointed and starting to get frustrated when he saw the tree line bordering a plateau of hard rock that gave upon an abyss.

He moved toward the edge, and saw a vast panorama of canyon and cliff that devolved into the Grand Canyon further to the East. It was spectacular, all whorls of rock with here and there hoodoos and other striking formations. He wondered why the doofuses in the government hadn't taken it over and made it a monument or nature reserve or some such other bureaucratic name that meant, bottom line, land grab. Cutting down space with barbed wire or some half-ass signpost that said US gov, that's how it had gone in the country for some 200 years. A few patriots remained though, and even if he hadn't been one until short weeks ago, now he had a cause.

Danny G lingered a moment at the cliff edge. The scene reminded him of a most unpleasant memory when a bitch had surprised him and almost sent him to this death. He had a score to pay, and the more he thought about it, the angrier he got. He almost made up his mind to head off right now by hook or crook to the South Rim, the hell with blowing his cover, and take out the bitch who'd sent him flying, totally because he'd been snookered.

But he wouldn't be again. Next time she'd go over the rim and if his luck held out, land on a cactus. He would relish hearing her screams. That of course, wouldn't last long, but some would be enough for a beautiful memory. And then Ranger boy would come next, if he'd managed to survive his bullet. And by the way he would be the first who did, survive one of DG's bullets that is.

When he turned and headed back in to the forest, Danny G realized in a flash he'd been too preoccupied with revenge to fully concentrate, or he'd have seen right away the backpack leaning against the trunk of a towering pine.

It was some distance away, but it stood out and he wondered how he'd missed it before. Could be the nature pussy had caught sight of him, dropped the pack and run like hell. As well he should. But he wouldn't get far, now that Danny G had locked on to his flight path. He'd be run to ground and gunned down.

When Danny G approached the pack, he noticed that it was full, which squared with a long hiking trip, and that a duffel bag lay beside it. He wondered why a hiker would add cumbersome weight and baggage like that, and leaned down to check it out, first peering all around to check surrounding terrain. And because he knew what he was doing, and maybe the hiker didn't, he scanned upward, to counter the old ploy of climbing trees, then pouncing.

Nothing up there but a curious squirrel, probably hoping like hell that Danny would leave to his, the squirrel's, devices the pack and all its sundry contents.

Danny G opened the duffel, and as he did so, felt the point of a knife blade on the side of his neck. A big blade, he saw out of the corner of an eye.

"Yeah, can cut your head clean off," the knife-wielder said.

"You ain't got the balls."

His quarry pushed and drew blood.

"We can cut yours off too. Let the gun fall."

Danny G hesitated, but the knife went deeper and he gasped, the pain almost as sharp as the blade.

He dropped the rifle.

The man behind him made no move, so Danny G made the first of his attempts to out-psyche: "You can't be telling me you hid and slid behind that tree. That's a cartoon trick."

"Worked."

"Once in a thousand times. You're crazy, man."

"The word is, 'insane.'"

Danny G turned slowly to face him and Zane let him.

"Ranger Rick. Damn. What asshole doctor spent government money sewing you up?"

"Maybe you'll meet him, fix that little cut you've got on your neck."

"Drop that knife and we'll see what you can do, mano a mano."

Zane slammed the knife into the tree.

For a moment Danny G didn't believe his good luck, that after all he had a fighting chance to get free and take care of the man who'd been instrumental in foiling him.

He swung.

It took only a few minutes. Zane Bailey not only had a body wired like steel cable, he'd learned self-defense on the mean streets of Los Angeles, and not a few martial arts.

While Danny G regained consciousness, Zane took care to bundle and truss him and organize his own gear. He strapped the rifle to his pack, as well as the duffel. He was loaded down but the ounces and pounds would soon be offloaded.

"I was insane enough to think about sneaking in to Hood's fascist Disneyland and taking you there, that little hut when your new lady friend finished scrambling what little brains you've got. Yeah, I got binocs. But lucky me, you came right into my web. Luck like that doesn't happen every day, so let's don't waste time."

He helped Danny to his feet. Some of Danny G's cobwebs had cleared, and Zane pushed him forward.

When George and Jimbo exited their part of the forest, empty-handed or course, their disappointment at disappointing their boss turned to panic in George's case.

As much as he'd been one pissed-off dude when he'd had his 4x4 commandeered and keys stolen, Marshall Hood had gone him a hell of a lot better in the pissed-off department. His ass had almost been grass.

No more "almost."

Because no more 4x4.

"What do we do?" Jimbo asked.

"Me, I'm walkin'. Crawl or walk, take your pick."

The 4x4 was at just that moment rolling into North Rim Ranger headquarters. Janey was waiting for it, flanked by Chief Officer Meyer and his two best law enforcement Rangers.

It wasn't every day that they saw a driver pull the vehicle to a stop and carefully, quite carefully, open the door and step down, under the knife-wielding surveillance of Zane Bailey.

"Some muzzle you got there, Mister G," Janey ironized.

It was in fact a large Ponderosa pine cone bound fast to Danny G's mouth by a large piece of duct tape.

"The head Ranger's talking to you," Zane said, "be polite."

He ripped off the tape. Danny G grimaced and recoiled in pain. As if he hadn't been beat up already, he now had a new facial scrape to recover from.

"You can recover in jail," Janey said.

"Bastard stole the car and kidnapped me," Danny managed to squeak out.

"We call it citizen's arrest," Janey corrected.

Officer Meyer countered, "Marshall Hood says different. Says you pulled a lot of wool over his eyes and we can lock you up for grand theft auto."

"Saving his ass."

"Not yours, that's for sure. This time we're keeping our eyes on you," Zane said as the officers cuffed Danny G and led him away toward a waiting Park Service car.

"I escaped once and I'll do it again," Danny G yelled back. "Your little lady's never gonna sleep safe."

"Last time I looked, she was kicking your ass," Zane yelled back.

Mercifully, Danny G was stuffed into the car and driven off, bound for a less than comfy jail cell.

"I'd ask how you did it, but maybe you don't want to tell," Janey said to Zane.

"Jupiter's luck," Zane smiled. "It was about time I had some. Maybe it takes getting shot. Thank Chief Wilson for his kind offer of a ride back but I'm a private citizen now."

"He was coming in his private vehicle. Guess he's sentimental. Or grateful."

"I'm going to do the traverse. Unwind you might say."

"Careful you don't love the Canyon to death. Yours."

"Good way to go, yes?"

"Someone's been calling, asking about you. Shall I tell her you're back? Or…"

"If she interrupts her work and meets me at the South Rim trailhead, I'll know the world has changed."

"The world hasn't. Sounds like yours has though."

# Rim to Rim

Despite every offer of a mattress, bed and clean sheets, Zane camped that night under the stars. Under a new moon, he saw so many it almost "drowned my eyes," he thought.

The next day he set off on the North Kaibab Trail before first light and had the delightful pleasure of watching every ray of the morning sun's light flash, constantly changing as he descended and rounded bends and moved deeper down into the Canyon.

He was in advance of the first mule train and had the trail to himself, except for the occasional Iron Man or Woman who ran by, trying their best as he did to avoid the droppings that fertilized the soil here, there and everywhere. Zane Bailey minded their leavings not at all. For him they represented life, and he thought to himself, I've just helped incarcerate someone whose droppings in word and deed polluted the environment much much more. Good riddance. And if the said person got out of prison in 20 years, he hoped and trusted Zane Bailey would be there again to monitor his moves. They would need to be monitored.

But in the meantime, he had the beauty of dawn and early morning at the Grand Canyon to keep eyes and soul fresh and happy. He walked slowly, contrary to his usual pace.

Savoring.

When he finished the descent to the Canyon bottom he was alone, no runners, no other traipsers.

The sun hadn't reached high enough to fully brighten the traverse, so he hiked along in a particular kind of half-light that despite the numerous times he'd crossed from north to south and vice versa, he hadn't experienced. Like life, he thought. Always changing, always bound to surprise at one time or another. He'd had one a few days ago. Could it be that she'd changed the way he saw the world now? No, he assured himself for what that was worth, I believe in what I've always believed and not transformed into a mooing and cooing Romeo believing Juliet brought the sun.

When he reached flat earth and began the long traverse toward the Colorado, he kept wondering.

He took the side trip up to Ribbon Falls and took a morning bath under the cascade. It was quite cool and a shock to the system, but salutary, bracing, a joy. After he'd gotten acclimated, he just stood under the water, letting it wash the dirt and dust and sweat, but not the thoughts and reflections and new feelings.

As many times in his life, he asked if he could forsake humankind for pure primitive wilderness. Himself and the wild, in the wild.

He wondered it especially now. He was alone but not alone, depending on one woman and her heart's desire. When he looked around now at the great Canyon he'd explored before, and often, he realized that yes, he'd changed. Or been changed. Now he was seeing and experiencing it through what could only be called the prism of love.

Many men and women in history, if not all at one time or other, had looked through this sort of prism. Probably they had all felt the same sort of surprise and gratitude. But did they feel it as deeply as he did now?

As no definitive answer came to mind, he decided to stuff the question into a side pouch of his backpack and move on.

At Cottonwood Campground he had detoured around to the back and the cliff face where he'd encountered the careless hikers who'd precipitated his recent suspension. He'd come once before after the so-called "altercation" to scatter and bury the ashes of their bonfire, and he was pleased to see that few if any traces had resurfaced. A burn mark stayed on the cliff wall against which they'd piled wood and brush and burned what they firmly believed would be their heart's content, fueled by several bottles of gin and vodka.

It was impossible for park Rangers to patrol and survey all the thousands and thousands of Canyon backcountry acres, and at any moment the risk of wildfires started by careless visitors remained ever present. True, he admitted, the danger rose exponentially on the Rims, especially the deep-forested North Rim, but here on the Canyon bottom it would have been a tragedy in his opinion, and most others, to see the desert cactus and ocotillo and yucca gardens fried to a blackened crisp.

He'd patiently explained this to the three gentlemen who'd set the fire, particularly the most vocal, a gentleman named Matt. Zane thought his accent and belligerence placed his origins on the East Coast, perhaps New York.

But at that moment, he doubted New York would be proud of him because Matt, instead of heeding the Ranger's cautions and emphasis on the rules forbidding open fires in the Grand Canyon, piled more wood onto his conflagration.

"Textbook open defiance," Zane explained later to Clarence Hillis.

"It's started, man," Matt had declared, voice rising defiantly. "Can't stop the music, know what I'm saying?"

"Strictly speaking, you weren't on duty," Clarence had said.

Truth. Zane had camped near the campground on one of his nightly walkabouts. Normally Matt and his cronies would have never been spotted. Unluckily for them—but luckily for Canyon safety—they had been.

"That's one reason I did what I did. I was acting as a concerned citizen."

"More like the Sheriff of Fractured Jaw. That's an old mo-
vie almost as old as I am, before your time."

"It swelled up but didn't fracture. If you want to know the
truth, I pulled my punch."

Zane had begun kicking dirt on the fire. Matt saw this as a
provocation and raised one of his "logs"—Zane recognized
the juniper.

"What the hell! Don't make me hurt you, man!"

"Drop that, sir. It's a weapon."

"Damn right it is. Want to see?"

Matt had come forward, waving it threateningly, close enough for Zane to recognize the fuel behind his reluctance to
listen, though he wasn't able to distinguish if it was the gin or
the vodka.

He knew for a fact however that Matt had indulged freely,
because when he punched him in the gut, some of the liquid
came gurgling out.

It took a while for Matt to recover breath, his guts emp-
tying to a high degree.

Zane used the time to further extinguish the fire. Matt's
comrades did not know how to act. Zane kept an eye on them
as they waited for their ringleader to come around.

When he did, his fury exploded.

"Back off," Zane said.

"The hell I will!" Matt said, charging forward. It was then
that Zane punched him out. Pulled or not, it was highly effec-
tive, knocking Matt out cold.

Politeness not now on the program, Zane turned to Matt's
friends. "What's it gonna be, guys?"

He stood face to face, confronting them. After a moment,
one of them shrugged and said, "We told him it was illegal."

"It is," Zane agreed, "let's put it out. When it's extinguished we'll wake him up and you boys can go back to your party."

They'd put out the fire together and Zane thanked them for their good citizenship.

They'd had to use some precious drinking water to revive Matt. Zane said, "Take a hike up to Ribbon Falls tomorrow. It's fun and it'll clear your heads right quick. Great elixir against a hangover."

Matt had glared and glared but had little to say. Perhaps due to an aching jaw.

As Zane bid good night, he said, "I'm camped not far away, as you might have guessed. Any questions or concerns, don't hesitate. Good night."

Zane knew he would be suspended, concerned citizen or not, and Clarence Hillis had confirmed that.

"Kind of an obligatory thing," Hillis had said. "Despite the actions one might characterize as in a good cause. Kids shouldn't play with matches."

"Yes sir."

"Now that you've got some free time, have a beer. It's on me."


Nearing noon, Zane arrived at Phantom Ranch and the Colorado River. He lunched there and enjoyed watching river, rafters and hikers.

He took the Bright Angel Trail because he was in no hurry, and it being longer than the South Kaibab, he would have more time to enjoy and bathe in the pleasure he was taking in life, nature, sun and desert, and very possibly, love.

As a child he'd happened on a book about Brighty of the Grand Canyon, the faithful and hardy mule who had spent his life ferrying tourists up and down the Canyon. Besides the pleasures of the book and natural sights it described, whetting appetite for the Canyon, he'd saluted the generosity of spirit that had led the early denizens and caretakers who'd chosen to name this principal trail for the Bright Angel who'd done his job so faithfully and well.

And those caretakers had kept it so. Once he'd said to Muir Wilson, in one of his more acerbic moods, that he feared one day they'd change the name to "Exxon, after they tossed some big bucks at the Park Service and paved the trail all the way down."

"Why not?" she'd said, provoking him no end. It still pissed him off that she hadn't immediately retracted the comment. Fortunately he'd been able to overcome his pissed-offness. Their trip together helped. But it was clear she still needed some rehabilitation.

At Havasupai Gardens he snacked and eyed curiously the crisscrossing hikers. Most showed the strains of effort, but he was glad to see that most also showed signs of deep satisfaction at having made it to the Gardens.

That was one purpose of the great national parks. Bathe those who dared to plunge in the world as it once was, and he hoped would always be. But he had many doubts.

From time to time he encouraged the panting and suffering. It occurred to him he was simultaneously decompressing from the wilds, his wonderful trip with Muir, his adventure on the Strip, and preparing for his reentry job as park Ranger.

He was ready. He couldn't think of any other job that would satisfy him, or that he could do as well. He just hoped that no miscreant tourist would get in the way of his fist.

He took his time and arrived at the final ascent of the Bright Angel at sunset, when the golden hour truly seemed golden this particular evening. The reds and golds seemed particularly bright and lucent, as if some heavenly artist had drawn them with highlights. Which actually, he thought, was the case.

Most people struggled ascending the Bright Angel, even if it was the easier of the two main South Rim trails, but he was happy to find that he still had enough vim to do it without excessive sweat, toil and trouble, even it was still just days after his severe wounding.

He doubted that Muir would be there, hanging out to see when and if he'd make it to the top. She knew him, and he knew that she knew he would make it. And also that if she did come expressly to greet him, he might get the foolish idea that she loved him. And she'd be stuck.

He knew she wouldn't give him that pleasure. She and he had had too many blowouts and disagreements, and they wouldn't end any time soon. Their trip had been a onetime thing, over and done with. Now it was back to reality. Romance came, and then romance went, like the variable Canyon winds.

When he got to the last stretch of the Bright Angel, he knew he'd look up and see the warm wooden lodge construction that meant civilized comforts, and though he reveled in and loved the outdoors that he really and truly considered great, he didn't consider it a contradiction to anticipate a nice glass of wine at the El Tovar bar, accompanied or alone.

He expected the latter, but as he made his final approach—most hikers said, "slog"—he heard voices, quite a lot of voices. Like some tourist party was clogging the trailhead and interspersing the customary oohs and aahs with commentary. Unlike some others, he never tired of hearing their wonderment at the glories of the Grand Canyon. It merited as much commentary as humans were capable of.

Now he saw though that the chitchat had a different tenor, because it was being generated by a whole bunch of his colleagues, among whom was his boss, Blake Wilson.

"They say the last step's the hardest," Blake yelled down. "You got it in you?"

"Hell yes!" Zane said, and his colleagues Lincoln, Lucinda, Lily, Josh, Harvey, Raymond and all the others joined in applauding.

He kind of thought it was because of his exploit capturing Danny G, but time would tell. If he managed that last step. Looked like for sure he'd be working as a Ranger again. The thought gave him energy.

It helped too, and happily, that among the group was a person not wearing Ranger garb, but the high heels and chic fashion of a real estate saleswoman. He'd have preferred she wear hiking shorts and a bandana, one with the lovely pinyon pine filigree he'd promised to buy her when they got back from their hiking trip and he'd finished his detour.

Yet another little bit of contention, among so many. No doubt she couldn't resist the peer pressure to come along with the meet and greet party, and didn't bother at all to take time to change, not wanting to give him the satisfaction of bowing to his clothes preferences. She had her own life and preferences, as she had, and would, endlessly remind him.

But looking up at her waiting there, smiling like she was despite herself and their conflicting views, the foolish and astonishing idea he'd had previously once again surfaced, that after all she might indeed love him. At least, sometimes.

"What brings you here?" he asked her with a smile.

She nodded toward the others.

"Peer pressure. And they're paying for champagne at the El Tovar."

"In that case…"

He took the last grateful step up onto the South Rim of the Grand Canyon, toward her.

*Martin Copeland is a screenwriter, playwright and author of* THE BOYS FROM DOGTOWN, RIVER OF DOUBT, MANHUNT IN FRANCE *and* LA LOVE STORIES. *He lives in Paris.*